One of nine children, Bess Ross was born in the fishing village of Hilton of Cadboll on the Moray Firth coast in 1945. Hard times for her family forced her to leave school early, to earn a wage working as a domestic in Edinburgh, until she returned home to Ross-shire and got married. Three children and one grandchild later, she went back to Tain Academy to work for the exams she had earlier missed; it was during this time that the first Neil M Gunn writers competition was held, and she thought: "I could do that," she did, and was flabbergasted to win. Since then she has not looked back. Ross and Cromarty Council Writer in Residence, Aonghas MacNeacail "made me see that writers are quite normal people, really, and that I too could be one."

Gunnie Moberg is a Swedish photographer who has lived in Orkney since 1978. Married with four children, her acclaimed award-winning work has appeared in numerous publications including *The Orkney Story, The Shetland Story, The Loom of Light*, and is exhibited internationally.

Other than that of the author herself, none of the photographs are of the people described in these pages.

cover photographs: Gunnie Moberg

A BIT OF CRACK AND CAR CULTURE

A BIT OF CRACK & CAR CULTURE

and other stories

Bess Ross

with photographs by

Gunnie Moberg

BALNAIN BOOKS

This book is for my sisters and my brothers.
"For auld lang syne."

Printed and bound in Britain by Billings and Sons Ltd,
Worcester.

Design by Sarah Fraser

The publisher gladly acknowledges subsidy from the Scottish
Arts Council towards the publication of this volume.

COMHAIRLE
Rois is Chrombaidh

2nd edition 1992

Published in 1990
by Balnain Books
Druim House, Lochloy Road,
Nairn IV12 5LF
Scotland

British Library Cataloguing in Publication Data:
Ross, Bess
        Main Chance.
        I. Title II. Moberg, Gunnie
        823'.914 [F]

(n.b.: *Main Chance* and *A Bit of Crack & Car Culture* are one and
the same)

ISBN 0-9509792-9-5

CONTENTS

Foreword	page 12
Mairac	16
Main Chance	22
I to the Hills	30
Footprints in the Sand	34
Twilight Time	44
In Dreams	54
Danny Boy	62
Once upon a Time, One Christmas	68
Empathy	74
Summer Visitor	78
Were You there?	90
At the Tatties	96
To Them that Hath	104
Old Johndy and Little John	108
A Love Story	118
Party Plan	136
Progress	144
Tearlach's Murdo	150
A Bit of Crack & Car Culture	158
Out to Search for Gold	166

F O R E W O R D

A Bit of Crack and Car Culture is not a novel. It is, however a village of stories. It creates a community of lives (and deaths) in an imaginable place. These are real lives, people engaged in the day to day struggles, joys and vanities of life.

Bess Ross is a remarkable writer, not because of her undeniable gift for creating a scene, describing a moment, but for the way in which, having apparently kept her imagination securely locked in for the first forty-odd years of her life, she has burst into sudden, prolific song. The entire contents of this book have been written in little more than a year.

Footprints in the Sand is here, the story which won the Neil Gunn Memorial Prize in 1988. It was also the first story Bess Ross wrote, some months previously, while sitting in with fifth year pupils at Tain Royal Academy, studying for her higher English.

Since then, Bess has been a stalwart of the Balintore Writer's Group, whose sessions I try to attend as often as possible. A number of stories in this collection are familiar to me from such visits. *Were you there? The Summer Visitor* and *Main Chance*, with its wryly observed study of an ever-hopeful, if not always successful, opportunist – these and others are warmly remembered as fine pieces of writing, which required little if any critical comment, when she first presented them.

This collection is the first appearance in print of a new, fresh and confident voice, offering much good and varied writing. She can switch from the hilarious to the poignant on the turn of a phrase, without diverting us from the crucial thread of narrative. And always, there is the warm humanity with which she draws us into the lives and experiences of her characters. It gives me great pleasure to welcome Bess Ross to the register of Scottish writers. She is a distinguished addition to the list.

Aonghas MacNeacail
(Writer in Residence – Ross and Cromarty District Council.)

M A I R A C

It surprised me to learn that Mairac was only thirty-four years old when she died, as she had always struck me as being middle aged somehow. Certainly much older than my vivid mother who was ages with her.

She was tall for a woman, with a heavy lumpy figure. Like a bag tied in the middle, as my Uncle Dan would put it, though not unkindly. As a young girl I was fascinated by her legs. They seemed to be of a uniform thickness and, summer and winter, were clad in heavy lisle stockings which concertina-ed round the ankles. I'd look at my own skinny legs and wonder if ever they would grow to be like Mairac's when I got old. Her hair was always fixed up in some sort of bun, pinned here and there, but seeking and finding escape from every direction. Her countenance had the colour of a smoked haddie and indeed, in memory, there always seemed to be a cigarette dangling from her lips: the first thing she asked for in the shop in the morning, before the messages or papers even.

"Give me twenty Players, Alice. I'm dying for a fag."

In the end they did kill her.

"How's Mairac's face so brown looking?" I asked my mother one day.

"Filth," she retorted uncharitably. "A good scrub's what she wants," and she pushed the sheets through the mangle.

Mairac was also slightly hunch-backed, and as I stood behind her in the shop, awaiting my turn and listening to that rasping cough, I'd become transfixed, gazing up in wonderment and speculation and not a little fear as to what her back would look like under her vest.

And later, as I got ready for bed I'd perform all sorts of contortions as I tried to see in the mirror what my back looked like.

"Have you no got any lipsticks for me? Rudd ones," she'd ask me, while I waited with barely concealed expectancy to see if her cigarette would fall from her mouth.

I shyly replied in the negative, not looking at her big brown face, but keeping my gaze concentrated on the packets of Persil, which were stacked to the side of me, near the counter.

"Well, ask your sister if she has any. She'll have plenty. And necklaces. I'm awful fond of jewellry." And as an afterthought, "Ach, you can serve the bairn, Alice. Her mother'll be waiting. I'm no in a hurry." This last was sprayed rather than said, as a paroxysm of coughing took hold of her. Her cigarette went up and down like a piston. It was the best I'd seen yet.

I blurted out my messages to the ever-smiling,
ever-patient Alice.

"Three pies, a jar of Blanco and the paper please."

The transaction completed I picked up my groceries and made a hasty, self-conscious exit, performing
a sort of two-step with Willa Jock in the doorway.

"What now, what now!" exclaimed Willa, jocularly.

I fled.

Mairac shouted, "Mind now!"

On my return home my mother enquired from the
back place, where she was making the tea, if I'd had to
go to London for the pies. So I told her.

"Mairac was in and she's asking if Grace has any
lipsticks or necklaces for her."

"Hmf – lipstick! She needs lipstick." This was delivered with heavy sarcasm, the meaning of which I was
too young to understand.

My father, from his chair by the fire, now spoke in
the soft, quiet way that he had.

"Oh you may scoff, Lily, but she wasn't always like
that. She was a fine looking girl in her day." And he
tapped his pipe on the edge of the grate. Reaching up
to the mantelpiece for his tobacco tin, he spoke as if to
himself. "Life's not been easy on her. That father of
hers. He was an old devil, a cruel man to his own."

"If she was such a fine looking girl why isn't she
married," my mother asked archly. "I don't suppose
any man would look at her," and she set the pies to
warm by the fire.

My father had resumed his seat and was puffing
away contentedly on his pipe. "Yes, and do more than
look. How slim she was. And the bonnie hair on her.
Hanging right down her back. Like the flax. And I
always mind her shoes. Shiny and new, always. Like
herself." He stopped, as if he'd said too much, and
finished almost as if to himself, "No, she wasn't always

like she is today." My mother cut the conversation
dead by asking if anyone wanted anything to eat, and
we took our places at the table.

That was the last time I heard Mairac mentioned in
our house. Over the next two years I saw as much of
her as I always did, usually at the shop. I tried to keep
out of her way as much as possible in case she'd collar
me and ask where her lipsticks and necklaces were.

Then she died.

Some days after the funeral a few of us were on the
shore looking to see what the wild seas of the past few
days had brought ashore, when we saw smoke rising
from Mairac's midden and the usual post-funeral
smell of burning clothes reached us. Mairac's brother
was there, prodding about with a stick, turning things
over in the flames.

We hung about on the rocks, pretending to be fully
engaged in looking for porstans and juntacs, all the
while appearing completely oblivious to man and fire.

As soon as the brother had gained the bank and
was starting up the vennel we dandered over to the
fire in the deceptively nonchalant way that was ours,
there to gaze mawkishly at what had been Mairac's
life.

The brother had made a good job of the burning.
There was very little left to see. Lying among the
ashes all that remained of Mairac were a round metal
buckle and a burnt out spectacles case. She herself
was now rolled flat and tidy in the cemetery on the
hill, above the village.

We decided to take the shore path home and it was
just as I was climbing the bank that I noticed the
photograph. It was lying beside an old lobster box
where the still fitful wind must have tossed it, out of
reach of the flames. Its edges were curling and black.

After a first startled glance, I hastily stuffed it up

my sleeve, lest the others should see and become curious and then playful.

On the way home I barely spoke a word, so heavy was my knowledge on me. Every step was agony. What if they should guess? What if − horror of horrors − it should slide out of my sleeve and land on the ground at my feet? In my agitated state I saw the whole thing played out before my eyes.

When the others had left me I stole round to the back of our shed, there to extricate and study my portentous find.

I found myself looking on the face of a young man with dark curling hair. He was wearing the uniform of the Royal Navy. The same photograph was in the big green album which was kept in the dresser in our room and which I liked to study on dull, wintry days.

And as the man in the photograph looked back at me with my eyes, something of my mother's strange attitude began to make sense to me. As I crouched behind the shed, watching the daylight beginning to fade and listening to the soft lap-lapping of the sea, which was in me and all around me, a great truth was borne in upon me.

Dusk had come for the daylight and with it was bearing away that part of me which slept on in wilful ignorance.

And with this knowledge my life had suddenly become something to be borne instead of something carelessly enjoyed.

MAIN CHANCE

Sanders Main was eighty-four years old when his son Uisdean came home from the sea and took the axe to the boat.

They were talking about it in the shop the next morning.

"Well, well, what's this I hear?" Finlay asked Johann Main as he waited for *The Fishing News* and half an ounce of Erinmore tobacco.

"And what would that be, Finlay?" she asked, jamming six rolls, a large box of paper hankies and a bottle of Lucozade into a plastic carrier bag.

"They're saying Uisdean put the axe in *The Gleaner*. Man, man, but that'll be the end of the old fellow."

"Old fool," Johann Main said shortly, her many chins quivering indignantly. "Nearly driving me as daft as himself. Do you know where he was at three o'clock in the morning? Down at the harbour. Trying to start the outboard and it in the shed this past two months."

She paused, struggling to regain her breath and, the tension almost breaking in her, said, "Well, that's the last time." She trudged to the door then hesitated to deliver her final word. "He should be put away," she proclaimed desperately.

"*The Fishing News* and a half ounce of Erinmore, Alice," Finlay asked the lady in the pink checked overall behind the counter. "What are you saying to that, eh?" and he thrust his hawk-nosed face at her.

"Quite right too," Alice replied emphatically, slapping his paper and tobacco on the counter in front of him. "The man's dited. Who knows what he'll do next. One pound thirty-six, please."

Drawing two soft dirty pounds from his trouser pocket, Finlay suffered to hand these to Alice.

Getting no joy there he left the shop and walked down to the harbour.

John More and his brother Donald were there. Donald was stooped over a bollard, making fast their boat, *The Good Shepherd*.

"Did you get any?" Finlay enquired of the dark-haired one. The young man looked up.

"Five," he replied through blue lips. "We put two back. Ach, they were only little things," and he used his hands to indicate the size of the lobsters which they had returned to the deep.

John More, on the point of disembarking, shouted up to Finlay.

"You wanting a crab, Finlay?"

"Ay, if you have one," Finlay shouted back, while

the wind, which was driving hard from the east threatened to shove the words back down his throat.

"One do you, or will you take two?"

"Well, two. I would take two."

The man in the boat looked perished with the cold. A man who carried no excess fat on his body, his neck had a bare exposed look, rising out of the oilskin which was many sizes too big for him. He now crouched in the rocking boat and selected two nice ones from the seething mass of crabs there. When he had gained the harbour Finlay spoke to him.

"Ay, she's a dirty day," he said with feeling.

"Ach, it's no bad once you're on the water," smiled the mariner.

Donald More had finished tying up *The Good Shepherd* and together the three walked up the harbour, carefully avoiding stray ropes and other men's creels, Finlay holding the crabs as if they were hot cakes, ensuring no part of his person came into contact with the mighty claws. The fishermen were quiet. In this quietness Finlay saw his chance and he took it.

"What about Uisdean Main then – what are you saying to it?" he queried, calculation hidden behind the bland expression.   The older, quieter brother spoke:

"Ach, he was a danger to himself, Finlay, and a tremendous worry to Johann. The woman's no fit for that. She's had enough," and he became silent.

Donald More broke in, louder, more voluble than his brother.

"If-if I-I was Uisdean I-I'd have smashed that boat long ago. He should have done it before he went back the last time and there would be none o-of this carry-on. God, the man's been senile for years." A wry grin spread over his dark countenance, and it eased itself into a deep-throated chuckle as he said, "a-as far as I-I could ever see there was always a jump in him." He quickly got himself in hand and, struggling to be serious again said, "No though, the man's a danger to himself right enough."

"Ay, right enough," agreed Finlay hastily, "But a man's boat, Donald? To go and smash a boat. I mean to say," and on a deep sook of his breath and a shake of his head he expressed his complete incomprehension.

"Ach," said Donald More, who was of a different generation altogether and had not the patience of his elders, "A boat's only a boat. Mind yon time, boy," he addressed his brother, "when we were all out looking for him, and a hole the size of your fist in her?"

"Oh, an awful man," nodded Finlay. "I mind – before your time it would have been – when the tyres on yon charabanc he had were bursted. What do you think the bold lad did? Stuffed them with straw. None of your tubes in them days."

"Well, I'm no thinking straw would have been any good for The Gleaner yon time," laughed John More.

The men had by now gained the bank and took their leave. Finlay was the first to speak.

"Well I'll tell the two of you this. I'm going to enjoy this crabs. They're going on as soon as I get in."

"Ay, they're beauties," said Donald More largely. "You'll have a feast fit for a king, Fulla," and his thought wandering in a different direction, "I wonder what herself has on the go the day?"

"Fish," smiled his brother. "This is Thursday, the day she gets the fishman."

They raised their hands in an unspoken farewell. John and Donald More crossed the road to their house at the foot of the brae while Finlay and the crabs made their way to the far end of the village.

Finlay wouldn't let the business drop. The following day found him down at the boatshed. Sitting on an up-ended lobster box, amid the accumulation of paint pots and fishing tackle, he turned his attention to Dan Wheeler. Dan had come down for a smoke of his pipe. His wife would not have the stinking thing in her house. Kept going on about her curtains and such like.

"But, right enough Dan, would you smash a boat? *The Gleaner* was a smart craft; now look at her. All broken," he mourned, wiping the drip from the end of his nose with a long, boney hand.

Dan smiled his gentle smile and lifted his bonnet to scratch his head. Replacing it he turned to Finlay and spoke.

"Well Finlay, in more as you might say, normal circumstances, no, no I wouldn't. But we all know how it is with Sanders this last while." He drew his pipe from his mouth and seemed to study it as he said almost to himself, "Since a good while. Did you hear about him trying to light a fire in the centre of the floor, the living room I believe they said it was, in the middle of the night?"

"No!" Finlay's mouth hung open like a mourchan, appalled that this juicy piece of news had never reached him at all.

"Oh but yo," Dan nodded. "The whole lot could have gone up I believe. Ay, Johann has her work cut out there," and he shook his head sadly.

"I never heard a thing about him lighting fires now," said Finlay and he moved his lobster box companionably closer to Dan's and prepared to settle down to some more disclosures. Dan however, would say no more and Finlay very wisely decided to change course.

He tried a different tack.

"But could Uisdean no have fished *The Gleaner* himself?"

"Be reasonable, man," said Dan, "what would be

the point and him never home for more than a few weeks in the year. No, *The Gleaner* was Sanders' boat and Sanders is no more as you might say, or near enough. So what Uisdean did was right."

Finlay was about to say more but Dan's nod towards the open door halted him.

Uisdean Main came into the shed and took a seat beside Dan Wheeler. He was a hardy looking man, tall and spare. No one could ever say truthfully that they had seen him wear a jacket. In all weathers the sleeves of his geansaidh were pushed up to reveal the anchors tattooed on each forearm.

The men exchanged greetings, discussed the big sea and the catches. Finlay stood up to relieve the ache in his left leg and made a show of looking at the weather through the open door. At his back Dan Wheeler was dropping him right in it.

"Uisdean lad, Finlay here was wondering about *The Gleaner.*"

"And what's that you're wondering, Finlay?" asked the sailor as he looked at him through partially closed eyes.

"Well, I was only wondering, like. Did you need to smash her? She was a fine boat I mean to say." A slight edge that could have been a whine crept in to his voice as he came out with it at last. "I wouldn't have minded her myself."

Uisdean Main's bellow could have been heard in the next village.

"Oh ho Finlay, I get you. Out for the main chance as usual. Sorry man, but she had to go. That was the way of it." He finished with a deep sadness.

"Ay, ay. Right enough," nodded Finlay, letting the thing go at last.

"And I'll tell you something else," and here Uisdean Main's look raked in Dan Wheeler also. "I took the pedals off that damn bike. Where do you think we found him yesterday?"

In truth Finlay had not the remotest idea where they found Sanders Main yesterday and little would he have cared. He had tremendous difficulty in recalling where he himself had been twenty four hours ago.

He looked at Uisdean Main sharply and his ferrety look became subtly calculating:

"Oh man eh! Do you tell me that? That bike was near new. You wouldn't think of giving it off?"

I   TO   THE   HILLS

Rob drew his watch out of his waistcoat pocket and looked at it. It was now two o'clock. He wondered what in the world could be keeping her. Every Wednesday for the past six years he had been stopping here. Every Wednesday, bang on the dot of half past one. And sure as anything there she'd be, tripping down the lane to the van, as light and as lissom as you like; the summer sun, like now, turning her hair to the colour of the corn, her skin caressed to a honeyed richness by its rays.

As soon as she came in sight of him she'd raise her hand in greeting. Right from the start she did that. And from that distance he could read the smile in the open friendly face. He liked the walk of her, swinging along as if she barely touched the earth but floated somewhere above. And the basket of eggs on her arm: proud as proud could be at the size of them. And he had to agree. He never saw eggs the like of them. Not once. She'd laugh then and say that he was teasing her, but he wasn't – not always.

Her man there, ploughing up the field across the road, had always lived on the place. Rob had known him many a long year – ever since a boy, coming on the van with his father. Always a dour one, even then. Kept himself to himself. The father had the croft back then. Like father like son, they said. Whenever Rob passed him in the fields he'd give the fellow a wave and a nod and he'd raise his hand to Rob. Acknowledging him. Just that, no more. The mother was dead now, they both were. He went first, then her, about six years back. That was when the lassie appeared.

You could have knocked Rob down with a breath when he heard the news. No one had ever heard of him having a girl. Then one day during that summer he went off and came back with her. Married, they said. Well, it just went to show.

Rob thought that marriage would have softened him, opened him up a little, but not a bit of it. He went about just the same; saying very little and working every hour that God sent on that place, the dour brute. Gey poor company he'd be for that lassie, or for any lassie come to that. And her, stuck away out here on her own with no one to talk to but the beasts.

She talked to Rob – she never stopped – and the things she'd say... and he liked to hear her. About how she could hardly bear for to see the plough opening up the earth. It was like ripping a great gash in the belly of someone very dear, and the sight of it made her shudder. And the sky. Did he ever see such a sky? Did he see it last night? Up there you'd be on a different earth altogether... and the hills. With the changing colours on them. Red in the morning in the rising sun, then changing to dark blue later in the day – just like dark blue velvet. She'd talk about all that and more. It was oh Rob this... and oh Rob that... and he'd stand there, studying the changing expressions on the sweet face of her and warm himself at her laughter, the old fool, as he handed her her man's tobacco.

Rob looked at her man. Up and down, up and down the tractor went, his head turned round to follow the line of the plough. Rob saw that he had stopped and was lumbering over to the edge of the field and was shouting something across to him. He wound down the window of the van.

Well, he wasn't surprised to hear that she had gone. It amazed Rob that she had lasted so long – a lassie like that.

He'd seen the change come on her. Slowly it came. Imperceptibly almost, to begin with. Ever since that big shed went up around the back of the house. Blocking out the light and the view from her windows. When he'd be working in the shed and she'd be sitting there by her fire with her knitting or her books, she'd gaze out of the window enthralled, just watching the clouds going past. And in the morning, when she was waiting for her man's porridge to cook, she'd stand and look across to her hills, the great, beautiful, slumbering beasts. Always enduring. When she told her man those things he laughed. Just laughed. Said her head was filled with nonsense. But Rob understood.

And in the winter when there was little or no work to be done on the place at night, there he'd be, in that shed, banging and hammering away at who knew what and her just sitting there. On her own. And from that time the light went out in her.

Oh, I'm fine, she'd say when he'd ask how things were. And she'd still wave as soon as she came in sight of the van. He'd still tease her about the eggs. And she'd still respond... on the surface. But anyone with half an eye could see that the heart had gone out of her. Or had been torn out more like.

So, she had gone. That's what her man had said. With the big heavy face hanging on him. If once ever he smiled it would crack or maybe break altogether. She'd be back with her people, Rob supposed. He hoped to God that she'd stay there and that folk would be good to her. For if ever anyone needed it.

She had sworn to Rob that she got the bruise from the hen house door slamming against her in the wind. And the clothes which had framed her blossoming womanhood began to appear too large for her. As if they belonged to a different, bigger person altogether. No more did she come tripping down the lane, light as a leaf. But the smile was still there. Or something very near. His heart had turned queer on him when he saw that she wasn't coming. Daft that, now.

Rob had wanted to ask him there if everything was alright, but he wasn't an easy man. However, it looked as if there was something on his mind.

And no, the lassie wasn't with her people. They took her off to the asylum. Lord, the fright he got when he went home on Sunday night. The fire black in the grate and no word of a bite for him, a working man. And her sitting there, in the chair, staring at the shed. Moaning like a daftie. On and on she was going about someone shutting out the hills.

FOOTPRINTS IN THE SAND

The father was kneeling in front of the grate, trying to coax some life back into the dour fire. There was no heart in it; the coal was long gone and the heavy, damp logs smouldered grudgingly.

He was a man of infinite patience, gentle and easy, even with the wee bit flame in the bottom of the grate. A tall, spare man. His long nicotine stained fingers now poked a rolled-up piece of newspaper between the bars. He lit it and waited to see if the sticks would take. He blew into the fire. The flame rose bravely and then died.

The child beside him also waited. Her thin little body, crouched on the fender, had a desparate urgency to it.

"C'mon Da, c'mon. Get her going."

You were eight years old that winter and the first thing that anyone noticed about you was your hair. Wild it was, and red. A burning bush. It exploded more than grew from your child's head. The women of the village were always exclaiming over its curly beauty. You didn't feel very beautiful. All you felt was that you were always cold and always hungry. Right now the summer frock you wore did little to dispel the cold of that March day. The cuffs of your jumper were ragged and wet. You were always chewing them. You couldn't stop.

"It's no use. They'll have to go the shore."

Your father spoke over his shoulder to your mother in the bed by the far wall.One could see where the bairns got their red hair from. Her features were strong and sharp and she had a fresh, clean complexion. Wrapped in a blanket beside her was her new-born baby, her eighth child. An army greatcoat lay across the bed, its weight adding a warmth that the meagre blankets failed to provide.

You could see he was beat. He turned back to the child on the fender. She was now intent on having her go at the fire.

"Just try will you to get a wee puckle, like a good lassie."

"Och, why is it always me? It's always me. It's Sunday."

"Fine I know what day it is. C'mon now. You'll get a bag in the big cupboard in the closet."

You too, knew you were beat. Mutiny still stamped on your face you went ben for the bag.

He was now speaking to Jeannie who was on the bed, studying the buttons of the big coat.

"C'mon Jeannie sweetheart. Where's your coat?"

"Eeh, that bairn can't go on the shore with that

cough."

That was your mother speaking. She always called Jeannie *me bairn*. She never called you *me* anything but you didn't care. You were your father's lassie. That's what he always told you: "You're your father's own lassie." You loved your father and were always frightened for your mother. She was always sick when she got babies.

Jeannie was cute. Five years old and there was none cuter. She started coughing. Every time she wanted to get out of doing anything the coughing would start. Your mother's sympathy only made her worse, near strangling herself so bad her cough was. You felt like slapping her. Nobody cared about your cough or even your blistered leg. Boy, that was one time her cough didn't save her. She'd been told repeatedly to leave that teapot alone, she would burn herself. Her defiant little hand went out to lift it, she couldn't, and your left leg got the lot. You started crying, she started coughing and crying and in the sarachadh your mother skelped you. You danced outside to your father where he and Jakey were baiting the line under the lilac tree. He sorted you and told Jeannie that his tongue was thin warning her about that pot and that if he would once draw his hand she would know where her heart was lying.

You got your coat and your father finished buttoning you into it. Then he did Jeannie and tied on her pixie and scarf.

"Where's your pixie?" he asked you.

"It's in my pocket," and he tied it on you.

"Mind the bag now," and he came to the door with you. You weren't off yet though.

"Somebody'll see us," and faith! The whole town would see you, for who could miss that hair, and weren't folks always looking to see what they could see. Your brother Duncan said that Ronnie Skinner could see anything with his spyglass. Round corners even. He could see from his sheds right over to Black-rock and knew fine just who was cutting the corks off his nets and selling them back to him for threepence. Duncan knew lots of things you didn't.

"Now Elizabeth, mind Jeannie from the water."

He stood there, slightly stooped in the doorway. His bonnet was smeared with soot on the peak, testament to his set-to with the fire.

"Mind that one from the water!" She needed no minding for the shore was her natural habitat. She thought herself right smart because your father told her he found her in a cligh. You'd beg him to tell you where you came from and he'd tease you and say, well now, he couldn't rightly mind and you'd press him and he would say he minded now – it was when he was in the South Sea Islands and he found this poor little lassie that no one wanted and so he took you home on a big, huge ship. You liked your story far better than Jeannie's. Who wanted to be born in a smelly old lobster pot? You didn't.

At the gate you looked back. He still was there. You crossed the road, down the vennel and you were at the shore.

It was a wild blustery day. The bag streamed out behind you like a parachute and the wind seemed intent in rooting you to the spot. The bullet-gray sea was choppy; the white horses galloped madly across the firth. The sea was on the ebb, slurping and gurgling as it drained away from the channels between the rocks. The seagulls whirled and screeched like dervishes.

Duncan once bet you that you couldn't count a hundred passing the skylight window. You couldn't. He said that he could count thousands but you didn't believe him. You thought he was counting the same ones over and over.

Your plan was to go as far as the harbour. You'd gather your sticks into small heaps and bag them on the return journey. That way you'd have to hump the increasingly heavy bag one way only. Your legs, red chapped at the knees by the coarse wind, slipped and slithered in their rubber boots over the seemingly living mass of tangle and seaweed.

Davac was there, standing looking out to the sea and cried to you: "What now? Where are you off to the day?" and you told him. Jeannie hated when he called her Jeannac. She would tell him most pointedly that her real name was Jean Marylin and that she was called after a nurse that your mother had known in Newcastle. Oh, she was so prim. You felt terrible then for the poor man and him only being nice. You didn't care what you were called. You started life as Elizabeth, a right posh name. You were called after your mother and the Queen. Now you were called Bess after Hughie Patience's dog which was red like yourself. The two reddest things in the village! Only your father and your mother and the teacher called you Elizabeth now, so you hadn't much patience for my lady and her swank.

You said ta-ta to Davac and he told you to watch yourselves from the water now. You called to Jeannie to come on. She was down at a rockpool, turning over the big stones looking for porstans. Her pixie was off and the fine wisps of her red gold hair blew across her face, some of them sticking in the snotters which ran in a steady stream from her nostrils. Every so often her small tongue would snake out to suck in the corruption. The sleeves of her coat were sodden and you could see what was coming. She'd be coughing like a horse and you'd be for it.

She came grudgingly, squelchingly from the pool.

You'd gathered your first pile and were ready to move on. You'd managed to find a few good bits with lots of burning in them and some bits of coal. But sticks or coal wasn't what was on your mind. The shore was your heaven and you could be doing better things than gathering wood. Sometimes if you looked really hard you'd find a sea-cradle or the beautiful domed shell of a sea-urchin. You thought they were seals' eggs but your brother Jakey put you right. Jakey was seven and knew all there was to know about such things. He was your father's shadow, going to the sea with him for the bait.

The middens drew you like a magnet. And the ritualistic out- psyching of the other, the nonchalant *don't breathe what you've seen* kind of thing that went on. The barely perceptible lengthening of the stride, then the slow gathering of momentum, ankles buckling, breath bursting out of you, was like a piece of film played in slow motion. But the race was to the swift and at the first sign of a turn of speed from the other you were off. Oh, you were magnificent in flight, ripped sandshoes metamorphosing into Mercury's winged sandals. And then you were there, pouncing on that jewel of inky blue to find it was only a scent bottle. You thought it priceless anyway, a treasure to be stored away and taken out later and exclaimed over by Jeannie and her friend Anne.

There was nothing exciting ever at Mary Johndy's midden. She was an old, old woman and didn't throw out bonnie things. Johndy himself had a boat called *The Trade Winds*. You thought that a right fine name for a boat. It spoke to you of far away, magical places. You thought Johndy looked like the skipper on the sardine tin. You minded going with Duncan, Jakey and Jeannie to see them one New Year. 'Happy New Year', you said. 'Happy New Year', said Johndy and his wife, very respectful like, and shook your hand. Then herself gave you a sixpence and a glass of raspberry wine.

Across the road lived old Nanacky and it was there Jeannie wanted to go instead of doing what she was meant to be doing.

You'd gathered a fair amount. You'd be glad when you reached the harbour, glad to turn for home, to be in out of the cold wind. Jeannie was scrambling up the bank intent on reaching old Nanacky's and if once ever she went there you'd never get her out. Nanack'd keep her for hours, feeding her black striped balls and madeira cake smelling of germoline. You wouldn't eat her madeira cake for anything. Likely the cats would have been at it first. They were everywhere.

You caught the belt of her coat and yanked her down off the bank, ignoring her pleas for you to let her go. You told her she could carry the bag for a change and told her to stop girning, then gave her a pandrop and as a further form of bribery mentioned Dole's midden.

You wished you'd kept your mouth shut. She took off like a bullet. Well, you could easily beat her. You soon passed her and didn't let up until you reached Dole's. You stood there, bent nearly double, your breath forcing itself from you in short, sharp gasps. And that's when God spoke, nay *ROARED*, at you:

"Chase home! What's taking you to the shore on the Sabbath? Away home now!"

You knew you were done for. Knew it ever since you neglected to put your penny in the Sunday School plate the previous Sunday. Oh, you pretended you did, but there was no way you could ever fool God. He saw everything. He even knew that Will Tarrel took his shoes and socks off when he used the lavatory. All that week you were afraid that God would smite you and that one day you would wake up dead. Your prayers became garbled, frantic entreaties to God to keep you safe. You couldn't eat, had no call even for the pandrops your granny gave you. And just this morning you thought you had got past Him! You even put a threepenny bit in the plate to be sure.

But now, as your breathing was becoming easier and your heart was steadying, you dared to lift eyes to the direction of the voice, and felt cheated, for it wasn't God, it was only old Dole, your father's uncle. He was always chasing the bairns from the shore.

You took to your heels as if all the hounds of Hell were indeed after you. Jeannie'd long since scattered and would be near home. You picked up the bag which she'd dropped and began the systematic gathering of your bundles. Into the bag with them, throw it over the shoulder, the bag bumping against the back of your knees. Then on to the next and the next, repeating the process, the bag becoming increasingly less manoeuvrable. And still your heart wasn't right as you struggled up the bank, on up the vennel, crossed the road and you were home – open the gate, up the path and that was you.

Your father was at the door, Jeannie with him. He took the heavy bag from you and said "Oh laddie, but you did well; we'll just put them in the shed."

You looked at him at that, and he told you. Davac had guessed there was no fire when he saw the bairns on the shore and so had come in with a pailful.

You went in and they were all there, sitting looking at the fire, exclaiming over the beauty of it. Your weatherbeaten face and knees nearly outdid the fire's glow. Your mother looked nice and smiley. Your little new sister was asleep and your father asked your mother if she had an onion and oatmeal in the house. She said she had and your father, proud like, said,

"Now I'll show you how to cook." He was awful proud of his cooking... And as the skirlie sizzled in the pan the smell filled your nostrils and the room. Even your teeth watered and you felt all warm and safe inside and you wished you could hold onto such times and wrap them round you like the big coat on your mother's bed and hide inside them forever. You wished you could shut out those other times that made you head for the shore – afraid to return.

TWILIGHT TIME

Slowly, with the aid of her spectacles, Esther pushed first one, then two, then a third tea biscuit across the small table in front of her, while her other hand clamped over her wrist in an attempt to control the tremors that the effort caused. Then she banged noisily to attract the attention of the three old ladies seated near her and who were to be recipients of her generosity. She could feel Catherine's eyes boring into her. Well, let her look, with her large cow eyes. She couldn't upset her any more. And she wasn't having any of her biscuits.

Esther didn't like Catherine. She did in the beginning. She had thought her quite nice then. Being a friendly person by nature, Esther had looked forward to getting to know the new occupant of the chair to the left of her. When Catherine had stood in the centre of the dayroom that day, looking lost and a little afraid, and Nurse Baxter had said, "This is Catherine, ladies," Esther didn't hesitate to wave her over. There were several empty chairs but no-one had bothered to offer Catherine a seat beside them. They all just sat and looked. No, she was the only one, smiling brightly at Catherine to put her at her ease. It was Esther's way.

Della used to sit beside her. Della had sat beside her for nine years. Esther missed Della when she went. She still missed her. One day she just wasn't there and her son didn't come any more. Della's son always spoke to Esther. He was nice, he was a bank manager. "What's new Esther?" or "What's fresh, Esther?" he'd ask her. There was never much fresh or new with Esther. Just sitting there. Now there was Catherine.

Esther had just begun to feel herself easing into friendship with Catherine. Then she went off her. Just like that. She couldn't explain it except to say that Catherine got on her nerves. There was her over familiarity with the nurses, laughing and talking loudly with them as if she had known them a long time. Taking over the day-room as if she had the right. She was a very familiar sort of person Esther thought. She didn't like that in a body. There were just some things that you kept to yourself. There was the time she made Sadie feel small, sniggering with that Anne over Sadie's knitting. And then she had said, loudly enough for the whole place to hear, "I'm only thinking it's a net you're making missus, for a salmon." There was no need for that kind of talk. There was a nasty streak in Catherine. Little Sadie had just looked up at her and smiled, then drove the pin through the tight navy coloured loops. She'd shout at Esther, "It's the L plates you're needing on that thing, missus," making her feel a fool, as she

tottered with the aid of her zimmer and a nurse
holding on to her, towards the toilet. She could feel
Catherine looking at her with every slow, heavy step
she took, unnerving her. It was alright for people
who still had their faculties. Catherine had. She could
walk unaided and said she didn't need glasses. If you
could believe her. But she was still very slamp. Showing off, Esther thought. And she was a good age.
Bragging when she came in that she was eighty-seven.
Esther thought that she looked ninety at the least,
with all those lines. If she herself was a few years
younger she'd soon show milady who was slamp and
who wasn't.

Esther could still feel Catherine looking at her. Well,
she could look all she liked. A cat could look at the
queen. If she was waiting to be offered one of her
biscuits she'd have a long wait. That was all that
Esther was going to say. She was always at that, looking. She never said anything. She thought that she
could wear Esther down with her silent treatment.
That was her sly way. She'd wait until the coast was
clear before she'd start. Right now, one of the young
nurses was clearing away the water jugs and Mrs Poe
was in, doing the rounds with her trolley containing
biscuits, sweets and toilet things. Catherine was cute.
Esther would give her that. Out of the corner of her
eye she could see her egging on that Jessiemay.
Esther knew that Catherine had found a great ally in
Jessiemay. She was soft as clart.
     Esther looked at each person sitting there, looked
at the tropical fish in the tank. They were meant to
make you feel peaceful. Esther supposed that they
might, but how many of the others could see them?
She saw that some were looking at her, that Nurse
Warner had her eye on her. Why were they all looking at her? She was making no sound. If Warner

wanted to look at anyone she could start with these two beside her. That's where the racket was coming from.

Catherine got up, walked easily over to the trolley. Esther watched her. Swinging along like a galleon in full sail. The size of her. Esther had never seen anything as fat as Catherine. The nurses had their work cut out trying to lift her in bed. And she'd be giggling and laughing like a lassie, wakening the whole ward. And what did she look like with them little short frocks, showing her knees. In the early, friendly days she told Esther that she never wore big bloomers, she still wore little knickers. Esther didn't know how she dared. And her half dozen hairs tied up in blue ribbon, like something from Crufts.

That nurse had finished uplifting the water jugs and another had come in to take Flora to the toilet. Flora was a poor soul. She had no legs but she never complained. She was a good sport. She looked forward to the young nurses coming on duty. They were full of fun, catching her up in her wheelchair and birling her around as they raced up the ward with her, whirling her light frail body through the doorways in wide arcs.

Trembling with agitation, Esther watched Nurse Warner return. Tall, slim and stiff, she hesitated in the doorwauy, missing nothing, then went to sit beside Sadie to try and unravel her knitting. She tried to get Esther to knit. She didn't want to knit. She had never been a knitter. Was she going to start now? Knitting away as if their lives depended on it. Della could knit and she wasn't here.

Catherine had paid Mrs Poe for a packet of Rennie's and had gone over to talk to Else. She'd go round the whole lot, bestowing her presence on them as if she were royalty. She was patting Else's hand and Else kept asking, parrot-like, "Is this the Royal

Hotel?" She had been asking that since she came here and the answer still was 'no'.

When finally Catherine returned to her chair and sat down without looking at her, Esther decided that she would move to another chair across the room. She'd have the vacant one by the fish-tank.

Nurse Warner handed Sadie her knitting and came over to Esther, who was in the right form for her. You never knew where you were with that one, calling you 'pet' one minute and showing you up the next. If a person couldn't walk they couldn't walk and no amount of bullying was going to change that. She knew that they didn't believe her, but Esther had stopped caring about what they believed long ago. They weren't shoving her about.

Esther looked up at Nurse Warner and something in the expression looking back sent Esther scrambling for her packet of biscuits, clutching them to her spare breast.

"I want to go," she said to the nurse. "I don't want to sit here. I'll go there," and she pointed across the room.

"Now Esther, we mustn't go upsetting the others, taking their belongings. Now, you know that don't you?"

Esther knew that smiling look of Nurse Warner's. She wasn't fooling her.

"Come on now Esther. You know what I'm saying, don't you? Nod to me like a good girl." The nurse put a hand out to Esther.   "Give me the biscuits, Esther. They're Catherine's biscuits, not yours."

IN DREAMS

The cloud of big black flies hovered lazily above the dry rotting seaweed on the foreshore. The sun was in its zenith, baking the earth. The loud droning of a bee could be heard as it went about its business in the clump of wallflowers in front of the old ruined summerhouse. Far out on the silver sea a lobster fisherman was busy at his work. Voices of children at play hung on the hot summer air.

The two boys lay in the heat, their backs to the broken dyke. The days stretched endless and free and golden before them.

At twelve years of age, Davy was the older. As he drew on his half of the cigarette, hooded eyes studied the toes protruding from the worn sandshoe as, with one leg crossed over the bent knee of the other, his left leg scooped the air.

He was glad to be out of the house. His mother, for whatever reason, had gone queer on him this summer holidays. At every turn she lost no opportunity in telling him that he was 'running on it'.

"My word," she'd say in exasperation, "if ever a boy's running on it, it's you Davy Mackay."

How did he know the milk was going to boil over?

"Watch the milk," she said as she quit the kitchen that morning.

So Davy watched it. He watched it boiling up in the pan and flowing in a frothy stream down the front of the cooker. The rattler he'd received to the right side of his head on her return had threatened to loosen his back teeth. She chased him from her in vexation.

"Out of the house. Be going now. Away with you."

And it wasn't only his mother. Donald thumped him last night for taking his bike. The temptation was altogether too much for Davy. Donald's new bike was lying against the dyke, all shiny and alone. Not a soul anywhere. He saw his chance and he took it. He cycled clear through the three villages. He even took it down to the sandy bay and cycled as close as he could to the incoming waves.

Fear about what he had done did not grip his throat until he reached his Granny's on the way home. As he stopped to try to wipe the wet sand from the wheels with his sleeve he wished that he had never taken the thing, had never even seen it in his life.

Donald was waiting for him, the fury black on his face.

"Who told you to touch my bike?" he bawled when he saw Davy coming at Belle Johndy's.

Davy didn't have the chance to utter a word by way of excuse or apology. As soon as he dismounted, his heart leaping about inside him like a wild thing, Donald walloped him as hard as he could drive with his balled fist, right between the shoulder blades.

"Touch my bike again and I'll murder you," he added, the hardness in him unheeding completely Davy's loud wails and broken back.

....

Davy inhaled deeply once more on his cigarette, which he held between the thumb and forefinger of his left hand. He was aware of little John sitting beside him, trying and failing miserably to get the hang of the thing with the other half.

Little John looked at Davy through pale blue, watering eyes. Where Davy was large for his years and the colour of the berries, little John was Viking fair. His freckles had multiplied tremendously of late. So dense were they that very little of his fair skin was visible, except for those sun-burnt patches on his nose and cheekbones, which were peeling to reveal the tender pink layer underneath. A small stream trickled down each cheek. He was trying hard to be as good a smoker as Davy; he hoped he would one day. Right now however, it was a difficult business to master. Every time he drew on his cigarette he nearly choked himself. His throat would close up at the foul taste and he'd start coughing and gasping for his breath. Then his eyes would begin to water and he'd feel himself a right baby.

"Mammy's baby," his sister Ishbel called him. Sometimes this feeling of babyness would build up in him and frustrate him so much that he'd hurl his small frame at her and, arms flailing like windmill sails, he'd wade into her. At this she'd only laugh more and begin tickling him in an effort to draw from him the mood that was on him. Sometimes she managed this, sometimes not, and on these occasions he'd run out of the house, not caring in the least that he left the door wide open for the world to see in and, hearing her teasing laughter in his ears, he'd head for the shore.

Little John's admiration for Davy was total. Davy could smoke as good as anybody he knew. As good as his own father even and that was saying something. His father was the best fisherman in the place. And the best storyteller; he told little John many magical tales from the far away lands he'd seen. He was also the very best runner you ever saw. When his mother would call little John in for the night he'd hear her voice and run away from the house. His father would take after him and in the matter of a few long strides he had him. He didn't think anyone else's father could run anywhere near as fast as that.

Carefully, Davy stubbed out his cigarette on a flat stone and turned to little John, noting his distress.

"Och never you mind. You'll do it one day," he said knowingly. "Maybe by the time you're eight."

"Do you think so, Dave? Do you think I'll really be able to by then?"

"Oh at least," answered Davy, not bothering his high head about such details. And grandly, "Maybe even before."

"I'm eight after the New Year, Dave."

"Heaps of time. Look, give me your half and we'll keep it for again."

He took a stone out of the dyke and drew a matchbox from the cavity. In it he carefully placed little John's soggy half, replaced the box and carefully slid the stone back into position.

"I'll have to be going soon Dave. I haven't had my dinner yet. My mother'll be wondering," said little John, pushing the heels of his hands against his eyes to stop his tears.

"Well I don't suppose anyone'll be wondering

about me. I'll only get thumped when Hector finds out I took his last fag," said Davy heavily.

"He mightn't know that it was you, Dave. He might think it was Donald."

"Na. He'll know. I get blamed for everything in our house. Anyway, it's his own fault. Anyone could find them where he hides them – in my father's toolbox. Ha, ha. What a joke! It was his last one. I'll get murdered," Davy added philosophically as he plucked at the grass beside him. "Boy, when I'm working I can buy anything I want." And, the hope falling from him, "Of course that'll be a while yet."

"What are you going to work at Dave?" little John was breathless on entering this new world.

"Well, I'll tell you something for nothing. I'm never going to work at the farm like Hector. I might go to the fishing, or," the black eyes in him gleaming like jet, "I would really like to work in the garage in the town. And I'd save up every halfpenny of my pay and I'd buy a motor-bike like the one Charlie More's brother has. Did you see her John? Man! What a beauty! What power!" he finished, the ecstasy shimmering in him.

"Would you really get a motor-bike Dave?" little John asked, his breath almost stopping.

"Ay, and take you for a shot sometimes," said Davy. "If your mother would let you."

"And what else will you do when your working Dave? What will you buy after your motorbike?"

"Ten big bottles of lemonade at least," said Davy. "All for myself. And I'd hide them in the shed."

"What kind Dave? What kind?"

"I think six cola, oh six at the least. And two of still orange and two cream soda," and, the thing galloping away on him, Davy added triumphantly, "And I'd buy a tin of toothpaste. And a toothbrush," he ended with a flourish.

"Would you buy fags, Dave?"

"I wouldn't need to, man. I could still take Hector's."

"Do you know what's the very first thing I would buy Dave? The very first?" said little John, finding it hard to hold himself.

"What?"

"I'd buy my father a hundred gallons of petrol for his outboard."

"Well I think that would be a fine thing for you to do," Davy nodded wisely. "Your father would be awful pleased with that."

"And I'd buy my mother a real golden watch. Pure gold, Dave, with diamonds in it. Don't you think she'd like that?"

"Bound to I would say. That would be a grand watch to have."

"And although she does call me names sometimes, I'd buy Ishbel a large bottle of that scent stuff she puts on herself. I can't say the name. It's French she says. Maybe by the time I'm grown up I could manage it. What do you say to that Dave?"

"And what about yourself?"

"Och, I don't know if I can wait till I'm grown up for what I want Dave. I'm awful wanting a dog."

"What are you wanting a dog for? A dog's nothing. You can get plenty better things than dogs."

"No Dave. A dog is all I'm wanting. My own dog. A black one and I'd call him Ben. He'd have to be a sort of big dog. I wouldn't really want a little dog, although I might take him once I saw him. That's the way it is with dogs Dave – once you see them."

"If you had all the money in the whole wide world would you still only be wanting a dog?" Davy asked, astonishment in every line of him.

"Ay," acquiesced little John simply, the delightful thought shining from him.

"Och you're daft man," said Davy. "If you've money you could buy the world and everything that's in it. Don't you know that yet?"

"Well, I would just be wanting my dog. *Here, Ben, here Ben* I'd say. And my dog would come from wherever he was. Right off. Me and Ben could go anywhere. Anywhere at all. Right over to the big cliffs even."

"Ay, if your mother would let you," said Davy drily. He stood up, stretching his arms towards heaven. "Right, are you coming then?"

The fisherman had lifted his clighs and was making for harbour, his craft disturbing the mirrored surface of the sea, the throb of the outboard motor clearly audible in the still air.

Little John looked out to the sea. Saw his father heading home. The scent of the wallflowers was all around him, he heard afresh the buzzing of the bees, felt the sea rising in him.

"Davy," he whispered on a breath, the unbearable sweetness of it all hanging in his eyes, "Davy, what would you do if the sea was gold and the bumble bees were diamonds?"

DANNY BOY

Marjie knew that she heard the dummy speak. It was as she was standing behind him in the shop waiting for her mother's weekly magazine. He pointed to the shelf behind the shop-keeper and mouthed his unintelligible sound.

"Is it your Woodbines you're wanting?" the shop-keeper asked.

He shook his head vigorously at her and continued to deny that it was tobacco or pipecleaners either. Growing desperately impatient with her, he forced the word out, just as her hand was reaching for them.

"Matches."

He didn't say it, quite like that, as Marjie herself would have said it. She could say any word in the world that she knew. Without thinking. Her words were right there in her head and then they were out. Without trying. The dummy's words might also be in his head but he had to try. All his life. Even then he might not be able to say another word for as long as he lived.

Marjie wondered how long he had held on to that one. Did he know he was going to say it – that some-time today he was going to speak, in the shop? Did he have it in his mouth as well as his head ever since leaving the house, and did he hold on to it all the way along the street, repeating it to himself in case he would forget what it was he wanted, just like she herself would often do. For Marjie's mind was never where it was meant to be (that's what her mother was always telling her.)

Marjie had noticed the struggle that was in him, when Allie and Jamesy Jack were asking how he was today and all through the commentary on the weather. When Allie said, "Ay, it's a hellish day," Jamesy Jack, who was very holy, rounded on him and said, "And who are you, my man, to be going and saying that the day that the Lord made is bad." Allie took no offence, and as he skipped through the door with his loaf, thigh waders slapping at him, replied that he hadn't said that the day was bad but that it was hellish, as anybody that was looking could see, and that it was a boat that was needed out there.

The dummy stood there, slackly, with his message bag, and looked at them and down at Marjie and all that very precious time he kept his word in. She didn't know about his word then. It was only the dummy's usual harsh sound coming from his throat.

Marjie had always known him. He lived near them with his sister. She was tall and thin and her graying hair was plaited over her left ear. He'd come into their front garden whenever he saw her father about.

Her father always gave him his time and he enjoyed yarning with him. This used to puzzle Marjie's mother.

"How can you spend so much time with someone that can't speak?" she'd ask.

And her father would come back with, "Isn't it strange – them with little to say can spend all day saying it, and those with something in them, well, you never hear they're in it."

Without moving her head, Marjie let her eyes travel this way and that to see if any of the others had heard. Nothing seemed to have changed. The shopkeeper was in the act of putting the tuppence for the matches in the drawer. Her expression held no trace of wonder as she asked Marjie what she could do for her. The elder seemed to be still thinking that he could expect nothing else from a heathen like that Alastair Cameron. Marjie focused on the dummy. Even he remained the same. The same dummy who would go home to his sister and tend to his garden. He had given her mother leeks the day before. He had the finest vegetables in their village. He was very good at the wallpapering too and always helped any old person who had no-one of their own to do it.

Marjie took her mother's magazine from the shopkeeper, her gaze locked on the short round figure that was closing the door at his back. Once she reached home she'd be alright. There she could tell what she had seen and it would all be explained to her. She must hurry there, or she would shatter.

She left the shop and saw him ahead of her on the road, his head bent against the driving rain. She was young and quick and would soon catch up with him, but she didn't want to catch up with him today. Didn't want to see any more of him, couldn't bear to look on his face, see his mouth. And so she played about the pools until he disappeared from her sight.

She always thought of him as *the dummy*. That was the name her generation had accorded him. Her father detested hearing him called that, and was not slow to point out to anyone at all who called him that in his presence, that he had a name every bit as good as their own and would they mind that. That he was christened *Daniel* in the church over there.

Marjie knew all this and on meeting him when she was alone she would say, "Ay, ay, Daniel". But when she was running with the rest and they'd see Daniel coming with his tartan bag, which he always took to the shop, even for a small thing, she'd also cry that the dummy was coming. Not that she ever said out loud, but she thought it alright, and it was the same thing. Those who had wickednesses in them would run after him and taunt him about his bag or his hair. His sister used to cut it. She'd clap a bowl on top of his head and simply snip round it. It was judged that Daniel must have had little patience for this, as his dosan was invariably lop-sided, soaring into oblivion above one of his eyes. Marjie felt near to tears for him at such times and burned with shame for the part that she played in the whole unspeakable business. If her father had known he would think little of her. He didn't, for the thought stayed inside her, but that in no way excused her. She knew. And she knew that what she was at was wrong.

To those of his own age and to the old ones he was always *Dan man* or *Danny my boy* or just plain *Daniel*. These people never called him less than his name. That was the unkindness of her own kind. And the cruellest among them put fear into the hearts and minds of the little ones. They'd tell them that if they went past his garden in the dark, he'd jump out at them and grab them by the ankle and take out his teeth and his gums and show them the wide hole that was his mouth; and then, if they were brave enough to look, they'd see that he hadn't a tongue in there. The little ones would run home crying to their mothers, who had the job of putting them right and telling them that it wasn't Daniel they should be afraid of. Some wouldn't pass his house for anything, even in broad daylight and one or two would scream hysterically at the mere sight of him.

On the last day of the missionary meetings that summer, all gathered in the new stone hall to hear them. Daniel, the only adult among so many children, sat in one of the chairs in the front row, tight against the stage. Marjie loved the missionary meetings, loved to sing the hymns. She would try to take the roof off with her singing so that Jesus would hear her right, especially with the closing hymn *What a friend we have in Jesus.* When they finished, the missionaries handed each one an orange and a bag of sweets. There were those who said that Daniel had only come for what he could get, but Marjie didn't believe that. She knew that inside he was singing every bit as loudly as she was. For it was only in the eyes of the world that Daniel was flawed. On looking on Daniel, God looked on a perfect soul. That's what the missionary had told them. Her father had always known such a thing. He would say, "I know who's wrong, and it's no Dan."

As she trailed a long way behind him on the road home, Marjie knew. Today it seemed she alone had heard the dummy speak. Perhaps the only word he would ever speak. He had said *matches.* For her the most beautiful sound ever heard. And she knew that for a very short time back there, in the shop, with the rain battering on its tin roof, that she had stood in Eden.

ONCE UPON A TIME ONE CHRISTMAS

The canteen was situated on that barren piece of land between the villages of Balmore and Hilltown. Before it lay the shore and the rocks, behind it the bracken-covered rough grazing for Dalziel's sheep. A wooden building with a tin roof, long and low and black, it sprawled there like a large black beetle, clinging to the earth like a limpet to a rock. During the war years it served the servicemen stationed in the villages and outlying areas. Now, with the war a thing of the past, it was the village hall. Dances, socials and whist drives took place there. And, of course, Christmas parties.

In the living room in one of the main streets of one of the villages a mother was trying hard to groom her brood into some semblance of respectability. She had six children going to the party that year. That is if she could get them all ready in time, for a different kind of crisis had broken out. Margaret had been the cause of it and the feeling of disquiet was fast spreading through the others. She wasn't the eldest or the biggest, but there were times when she could cause more sarachadhs than the rest put together. Sitting on the fender, the heat from the fire turning her face to the colour of a lobster, she looked a completely new child altogether, shining from the toes of her shoes to the top of her red curling hair. Now, eyes that sparked their defiance, sent out their challenge as the stubborn child's mouth came out with it at last:

"I'm not going! I'm not going without a cup."

There, she had said it. She had always known that she would not be going this year. Last year she was five and when you are five you don't quite mind taking a jar to the Christmas party. At six, however, such a thing is not to be borne. The others could go with their jars if they liked, but she never would – everyone seeing your jar!

Her mother stopped what she was at, while little George squirmed and twisted this way and that and tried to dodge the rough coarseness of the face-cloth with which it seemed she would remove the top layer of his skin. He was the last to be done, and had whipped himself into a right lather whilst waiting, so keen on him was the anticipation of this party. His mother hastily dried his face and put him from her. Then she turned to the mutineer.

"Look – you'll get a cup when you get there," she said placatingly, "they've always got plenty."

The child still sat there, kicking at the edge of the rug with the toe of her left shoe.

"I'm not going! I want my own cup. Everyone always has their own cups. It's only the Beggs' that get cups there, and they're tinks. So I'm not going."

Her mother sighed deeply. She had been hoping that with them all out of the house for a short while, she could get the baby off to sleep and take the weight off her feet for a few minutes, for she was large with her eighth child.

"Why have you got to be so awkward," she asked. "The rest are all taking jars or getting cups when they get there." She sat down heavily on one of the wooden chairs, wearily resting her arms on the table. She studied her work-worn hands, as if to find some sign or solace there. Once more, she drew a deep breath and, brushing the heavy hair from her forehead, she pushed herself up from the table.

"Well, you can go, or you can stay, because if there's no cup there's no cup," and she reached for the comb for the little fellow's hair.

"Margaret's always girning, always girning. Jessie King never had a cup last year and she's no a tink. She just forgot. I bet they have hundreds of cups!" chanted Anna, three years Margaret's senior and the oldest of the girls. "And anyway, here's Da coming," she said as their father passed the window, "and you're for it, I'm telling." And on this last note she stuck her tongue out at the dissenter, only to be sharply reprimanded by her mother, who told her that things were bad enough without her starting, and would they be good bairns for their father coming in.

For their father had been out looking for work again and he had promised his children that he would bring them back holly with red berries on it. As in many other small communities during the post-war years, unemployment was running high in Hilltown and its neighbouring villages. Occasionally, the men could pick up casual work on the nearby farms, but during the winter there was little chance of this and for many families that old spectre, hunger, was ever present.

Their father propped his bike by the side of the house and unfastened a large bunch of holly with red berries from the carrier. He handed it to the oldest boy, with the warning to watch himself from the stabs; and, stamping the snow from his boots he went inside. Four children stampeded towards him, all eager to be the first to tell him the news. Anna was like a river in full spate, while little George took up when she stopped to catch her breath.

"Heesht now! Heesht!" their father exclaimed, throwing his hands up into the air. "Come on, in to the warm and be sure to shut that door for the bairn." And they all went into the living room.

Looking across the room to his wife, he sadly shook his head; the hope which had flickered in her eyes at his return, hung there a moment, then died. He walked over to the grate and stooped down to the heat, his hands out outstretched to the flames. He rubbed them together, held them to the fire again, and repeated the process a few times. Then he turned towards the child still on the fender.

"Well what's all this I'm hearing about ones no going to parties? What about Santa and your present?"

"I am wanting to see Santa, but I haven't got a cup," said the little one, holding onto her thrawnness.

"And will you no get one when you get there? Surely they'll have plenty."

"But I'm not wanting to get one. I'm wanting my own. The rest can get cups if they like. I'm not wanting one of their cups and I'm not taking a jar – I'm never taking a jar!" By this time the child was very near to tears and her voice had soared into the realms of opera. She hung her head once more.

"Well, well, if that's the way of it, that's the way of it," her father said as he straightened himself.

Wearily, he rubbed his 'hand over his chin and then the gleam came into his eyes as he seemed to reach a great conclusion. "I wonder now. I just wonder..."

His eyes snapped back to the child. "What would you say?" he asked of the downcast head, "What would you say if your father told you he could make you a cup?"

The head came up slowly, disbelievingly, to join those of the others at this fulsome statement. They knew well that their father could do anything. Anything in the entire world. Wasn't he their father? But – make a cup? Now that was a little difficult to comprehend.

Their mother meanwhile was engaged in changing their baby and amidst the nappies and mutual admiring that went on between the pair of them was unaware of what was about to take place.

The father was marshalling his troops.

"Now, one of you big ones," this man with a mission rapped out, "Up the stair to my toolbox. I want my soldering box and bolt. And don't drop it mind." And to his wife's bent back, "Could you put that marmalade in a dish. I'll require the tin."

She put the baby back in his pram and hastened to do so, while all gathered around the small table to marvel at this thing that was about to take place. Those who dared to venture loud protest that they weren't waiting as they would be late, were quickly quietened by those who would have waited an age, until bedtime at the least, to see their father making a cup. No-one else's father had ever made a cup, not ever.

Their father placed his components on the table on which a newspaper had been spread to save the table-cloth: One yellow tin with a golliwog on either side; one small piece of shiny tin, produced as if by magic from who knew where, out of which the handle would be fashioned; sandpaper to smooth the rim, so as not to wound a small mouth and the box of solder. The bolt was already heating in red hot coals of the grate.

Quickly he worked, for solder solidifies the moment it cools. On with the easily fashioned handle, a rub with the sandpaper to the rim, and the operation was complete.

"Now," the inventor stated hugely, "What do you say to that?" and he held aloft his prize for all to see. "A wash to clean it and there you are. What's wrong with that? I'll warrant you'll not see many cups like that." He turned to the child who had stood by his chair throughout the whole proceedings, her unblinking eyes completely concentrated on what was taking place.

"Well, what do you say? Will she do?" he asked of her, as she struggled with what was in her. He put his arm around her, drew her in to him. Then he said in a hushed, almost reverent whisper, "Get your coat on sweetheart. Quick now. Santa'll be waiting."

E M P A T H Y

My son woke like jagged ice this morning. He raised his head from the pillow and looked across accusingly at me from angry eyes. He has been like this for a long time. It is not by his choosing that he inhabits his world. Today, I can tell that he is in no hurry to enter it.

...I wish my mother would go away. Why does she stand there with that worried look about her? I'm coming. Can she not see that I am coming. How old she looks. And gray. Her countenance is the colour of early morning light. She is always there. I can never get away from her. She understands me more thoroughly than I do myself. There is irritation in my love for her. She is my other self....

My son hates what he has become. He does not be-
long to that world he is working so hard to be part of.
The greed and loss of self that exists in business today
is not for him. It does not let him breathe. Will not let
him be. He is fighting to remain himself. It is hard.
The continual pressure is to conform, to be a small
formless part of one whole. There are too many of
them. He is alone. I fear they will suck him in, turn
out a mindless clone, a company man.

*...I hate my job. I'm never going to like it. But it's
more than that. I'm not, and I'm never going to be
part of what it stands for. My mother thinks that
when I have served my time that I should leave, go
with another firm. Has she no imagination? Does she
know nothing? Everywhere it is the same. Young men
of my age backslapping and crawling their way up the
ladder of industry. I am horrified. They are all the
same. Why am I different? I have my own mind. I am
me. They will not mould me. Not for me in later years
director's lunches with drink flowing free. I am me.
How I despise the stupidness, or is it contempt, that
sits them drunkenly behind the wheel of a car. I am
young. My body is hard and strong. I am never going
to become fat-gutted with soft flabby white hands.
Like dead fish. Cold fish...*

My son was a golden child. I taught him to understand his place on earth. To know that every living
thing is as much a part of creation as he is. He is man,
guardian of the animals and birds... he is not better.
My son is not harsh inside. His is a deeper awareness
of creation than he yet knows. He is wild and yearns
to be free once more. He is a young warrior. Right
now seemingly overwhelming forces attack him.

...In just fourteen months I will leave my firm fore-

ver. *I will go out to see my world. I will learn the ways of my fellow dwellers. I will know them. Inside they will be like me. I will meet Thorvald in Norway, Valeri in Russia and Nelson in Kenya. We are all voyagers in search of the Golden Fleece.*

My father is the land. How strong and abiding he is Earthquakes cannot shake him. He is rooted to the earth. My mother is the sea. That restless movement is in her. Sometimes the sea storm rages within her, at other times she is calm. My mother has unfathomed and unfathomable depths.

I am both. The land and the sea have shaped me. I am fortunate and complicated.

My father taught me to wait. And so I have waited. It is three years since I left school and set out to join the human race. With hope large in my heart and my dreams in my eyes. I am angry. I am more angry than I can say. The human race as I have believed in it, does not exist...

My son is brave and kind. He is more sensitive, more intelligent than most. The child has become the man. He thinks that he is not brave enough, tough enough or deserving enough to be part of humanity. It is none of these things. The tragedy is that when he went forth to join the human race, the human race as he has believed in it is not there.

THE SUMMER VISITOR

"Oh ho! Will you look at what's coming," my father said from his stance at the window, where he was looking out to see what the day was doing.

"Come away," my mother said shortly, as she left the pot she had been stirring and joined him. "She'll see you."

I forced myself between them, and there we stood, like the inmates of an asylum, gawking at the woman making her way to our front door.

"It's Muriel," I said roundly and needlessly.

"Well, it surely looks like her," my father said, enjoying hugely my mother's discomfiture. "I see she hasn't lost anything anyway."

The words *Buckie drifter* floated unbidden to my mind but I hastily repressed the uncharitable thought. My father harboured no such lofty notions however. He turned to me and, rubbing his hand over the bristles on his chin said, "Do you think my chair'll stand her?"

I looked at him and saw the laughter which was bubbling up in me reflected in his brown eyes. My mother put a stop to the business by dragging me away and pointedly telling my father that he was no oil painting himself.

He quickly got himself in hand and, with a broad wink at me, while my mother's back was turned, said, "Now, now Maggie, we mustn't be unkind to the woman. I think we'll just be going to the shed," and with that he reached for his bonnet, clapped it to the right side of his head and crept towards the door, ignoring completely my mother's ritual tirade about his questionable manners and the lasting effect of them on 'that bairn'.

Half way down the path we met my mother's friend Muriel.

"Hello Muriel lass. How are you? Fine weather for your holiday," my father said.

"Hello Hector. I'm fine. How's yourself? How's the fishin' goin?" And to me, in the Glasgow accent that I found so hard to understand, "Hello darlin'. You stickin' in at the skewl?"

Before I could get my answer out my father was making his excuses for not being able to stay in for her visit and was already moving away.

"Just two or three clighs to sort, you know," he threw over his shoulder, "and then maybe we'll get the scountrach done. We'll see," and with that we parted company.

Glad to be out of a house full of women, my father gratefully settled to the task of repairing his clighs. The swift sureness of his hands as he transformed the balls of string into a covering for the lobster pots was something my eye had difficulty in following. I sat there, watching the long, bony hands at work: in and out with the needle, in, out... and the net flowed from his fingers.

Stamping his cigarette out with the heel of his boot, he looked at me in the way that needed no words and the pair of us did complete justice to "The Star of the County Down".

"From Bantry Bay down to Derry Quay
And from Galway to Dublin Town
No maid I've seen like the fair colleen
That I met in the County Down..."

"Well," he said as he finished the net. "That's that. I think we'll catch our breaths before the scountrach. Run you in and see if your mother has the tea ready, for surely their throats must be awful dry by now."

When I went in my mother and her friend Muriel had already had their tea by the look of things. They were sitting at the small table in our sitting room and my mother was reading the tea leaves in Muriel's cup; a practice of which my father was deeply suspicious and therefore of which he heartily disapproved. It was something she would never do in his presence.

I stood there in the doorway, catching the tail end of a conversation about a tall dark man. My father thought the whole business rather disgraceful, but of course what did he know – he was only a man.

"Well, don't just stand there. Come in and shut that door," my mother said catching sight of me as I stood there, storklike, the toe of one leg rubbing the calf of the other.

I shut the door and delivered my message.

"Da says he's wanting tea if there's any in it."

She slid the kettle back onto the flames and I took my seat on the sofa by the window, prepared to mind my own business.

Muriel was studying me in the close kind of way that always made me feel deeply self-conscious. I was very much aware that my freckles had multiplied madly in the last few months, that my hair resembled a burning forest more than the bush so described, and that my gannet-like eating habits were the reason for the best part of a pot of jam adding a rosy pattern to my jumper. Drawing long and deeply on her cigarette, Muriel exhaled, then spoke to me:

"You goin' to come first in the quali, hen. You come first and I'll buy you a bike."

At that I looked at her in complete disbelief as I tried hard to grasp what she was telling me. Did she know what she was saying? How could she know that I never stopped asking for a bike, a new one, but it made not the slightest difference. All we were getting was a baby and that was that. But now! Now, here was the chance.

I fully expected to come first. I always came first. I could beat any of the others. Hollow. Donald MacKenzie thought that he was great because his father was the headmaster, but he could only manage third last time.

A bike! Just wait till I told my friend Kathy, she had just got a beauty for the holidays. Shining chrome wheels, bright red frame (pillar-box red she said) and straight across handle bars. Not like my grandfather's big, black contraption. I could only go it by putting my left leg under the bar. And Ishbel was getting one when her brother came home from the Navy. And me too. Me too! Oh, it was hardly to be borne.

"And don't spill it, it's hot," said my mother, breaking in on me. "You can come back for your own."

I was in such an elevated state at my life taking on this new dimension that I could only gaze mutely at both women. Why, the world would be mine. No more to be confined to the village, I too could go out into the country with my friends. I'd often been asked but I never would go, not on the disgraceful machine that I had. But now! To see the farms all golden at harvest time. To be able to take off into the long, soft summer nights. And I'd look after my bike. I'd keep it like new, and no giving shots to anyone. No, none of that.

"Come on, girl, move yourself," said my mother.

Muriel, in fat well-off contentment sat there, elbows spread over the table, more smoke coming from her than ever came from the sheddie where Alicky smoked his haddies.

By the time I returned half of my father's tea was down my front and over my shoes. In my heightened state I found it difficult to make him understand just what I was trying to say.

"Now, now," he said, "Just calm yourself. There's little to be gained by hopping about like that," and he took his mug from me. "Just you catch your breath and then maybe, we'll be able to make sense of what it is you're trying so desperately to tell me. A bike you say?" and he took a gulp of the strong sweet tea.

And so, trying hard to steady my quivering breathing, I told him that if I managed to come first in the qualifying exam, Muriel would buy me a bike. It was true. That's what she said. Sure as death.

He took another mouthful and looked at me.

"Come here," he said, and I went to stand beside him. He looked into my eyes and I looked back at the strange expression in his.

"Muriel shouldn't have said that to you. No, she should not. She had not the right. When you take the qualifying exam I fully expect you will come first, for you have it in you. But you come first, not for your mother or myself; no, nor for Muriel and her bikes. Bikes is it!" and he almost spat the words out. "You come first for yourself, my girl. Now, always mind

that." And, sighing deeply, he added in a quieter
tone, "Now run in for your tea and then we'll see to
the scountrach."'

As I went back to the house I was in decidedly bad
form. Anger at my father for spoiling things seized
hold of me. Head down, I ploughed up the path. Any
pebbles that got in my way fairly got it. If one had
even hit the window, what would I care?

My father thought he knew everything. Muriel
would buy me a bike. She would! She said so!

My mother handed me my tea and looked quizzi-
cally at the state of my features. Declining anything to
eat I moped over to my seat by the window, not in the
least self-conscious now about those matters which
had weighed so heavily on me before. My mother
shook her head in perplexity.

From my deflated position I sat there, hugging my
cup. This time I studied Muriel. She could easily
afford to buy me a bike. No bother.

I eyed her large, bulging, cream leather handbag.
She had a wallet full of pounds in there. I knew.
Sometimes she'd open it and give me a sixpence and
I'd see in. I wished that one day she would give me a
pound. All that my mother ever seemed to have in
her purse were brown pennies.

Muriel was still drinking her tea and smoking. She
looked across at me, dismissively.

"You no goin' back to the shed, hen?"

I was glad to go. If my mother had asked me, as she
invariably did on these occasions, to show Muriel my
jotters with all the 'corrects' and 'excellents' I wouldn't
do it. Never. I'd take my schoolbag and run straight
out of the house.

Back in the shed, my father had started on the line.
Sitting on an old wooden chair, a canvas apron tied
round his waist and a plateful of lugworms on his lap,
his long fisherman's hands were unhooking the hook

from the cheepich, pushing the lug on to it and laying it in the creel. I sat down and began the unhooking process and passed the hooks to him. The line could have as many as four hundred hooks. He'd cast it in the evening and lift it the following day. It was a haddie line.

As I took my seat on my chair beside him, I looked at him, and he at me, and in his quiet, "never you mind" I knew that once more he was my father and that what he had said was right and true.

To know he was right the following June, when I did indeed scoop more than my share of the prizes, eased my pain not one small bit.

Muriel continued to visit my mother for many years after that, but never again was there any mention of a bike. The promise, it seemed, had been broken as easily as it had been made.

WERE YOU THERE?

Very few people ever bothered to attend evening service in the ancient Church, and that Sunday was no exception. The congregation sat there, all two dozen of them, in the centuries-old building which had been home to worshippers as far back as the Reformation. They listened in seemingly rapt attention to the quiet tones of the minister as he told again the old, old story of the Crucifixion.

He did not raise his voice to them now; he never did; did not need to. A man who gave the impression of deep spiritual wisdom, he spoke as if to himself, and for his text he was using the words of the old negro spiritual:

"Were you there when they crucified my Lord? Were you?"

He stopped and looked long and hard at his flock, accusingly almost. And again, more forcefully, the emphasis falling on each word, separating them, rivetting them home.

"Were you there?" And, as if he carried the weight of the entire world on his slight shoulders, he answered his own question with a deep sadness.

"Ay, you were there. I was there," and again that heavy, almost defeated emphasis, "We were all there."

A few shuffled uncomfortably at this. There was a nervous titter from somewhere at the back of the church. A sudden, furious rustling of pandrop bags broke out in the pews while the captive audience tried hard to get to grips with this verbal attack that he had fired at them. How on earth could anyone here have been at Calvary? That was nearly two thousand years ago. Heearn fhein, did the man not realise that this was the nineteen eighties? Och, he was off again on one of his convoluted theories. He was aye at that. Mumbling away half the time as if they weren't there. Who could follow him?

Feet shuffled once more. Someone nearly strangled himself trying to smother a cough. The sooner this lesson was over and they were on the last hymn and out of here the better. No wonder the church attendances were dropping. Them at Calvary! Now they had heard everything.

Davie Munro pushed another pandrop into his mouth and tried to still his coughing. The harder he tried the worse it got. God, it was so hot in here. It aye went for his throat.

He was wondering how He would get on under Maggie's Free Enterprise Scheme. All very well her going on about folk helping themselves, but how was a man to exist, when hardly anyone paid you on time? Was it like that for Himself back then in Nazareth?

Did He have bad debts too? Lucky He didn't have the
Council to deal with. He'd wait forever for them. Did
the folk back then boast that the mad carpenter from
Nazareth was an easy touch? Of course he was a
joiner himself but it was the same thing really. The
funny thing was that the ordinary people paid up at
once. Didn't want to be beholden. No, it was the big
bugs. You could whistle for your money for all they
cared. I wonder what he charged for chairs in Nazareth..?

Peggy MacBain shifted her not inconsiderable
girth. Her ankles were bad the night. Giving her gyp
they were. She wondered if Dennis would be in when
she got home. He left for the disco on Wednesday
night and who knew where he was since then. If ever
a boy needed a father. Came and went just as he
pleased and not a word about the worry he was caus-
ing her. And him with that car too. Every time he
praised its performance her heart leapt in her breast.
Oh, fine she could sympathise with Mary. She was
another whose Son took to stravaiging all over the
place. The Middle East, two thousand years ago or
hereaboots today, what the difference? And that
rough lot He went about with. That Peter fellow now.
A hot head if ever there was one. Ay, it was a mother's
lot. And Him likely no eating properly – where would
He get it? Always in the middle of lakes and wilder-
nesses. But Mary and Martha were good and true
friends. Just as well they were in it. He could aye go
there when He was aboot. Mary! Did He drive you
daft with his talk aboot sinners and repentance the
way your fellow did with cars. Car daft, Dennis! Oh
ay, it was a mother's lot...

Kathy Finlayson was dying for a cigarette. She
lifted the heavy blonde hair from the back of her
neck. Phew! The heating was full on tonight. Still, not
long now. She only came for an hour's peace and

quiet. Let him get the bairns off to bed for a change.
It's about time he did something. Did he think I got
them by Immaculate Conception? I don't know about
me being guilty of crucifying Christ but one things
for sure, marriage to that so and so is crucifying me.
Of course, I should have listened to my mother. But
oh no! I went mad to get him. Well, mad is the
operative word. If only he'd shoulder his responsibili-
ties, but everything's left to me. And here's Mr Ken-
nedy going on about Jesus shouldering the whole
rotten world. Oh, I'm dying for a fag...

The minister drew the lesson to a close on a broken
whisper. The offering was collected and blessed and
the congregation rattled through the last hymn,
drawing away from the organist in the home straight,
to finish by a clear length.

After benediction they galloped their uncomfort-
able way out of the church, barely taking the time to
shake hands with their minister on the way.

Once outside, bursts of light-hearted, nervous conversation broke out all around. Sighs of relief that
that was all over. He was coming on awful strong the
night.

Already cars were leaving the car park, popular
music issuing forth from the radio cassettes of some.

Marjie stood there, among the gravestones of the
long dead, and she knew with a sudden, startling
clarity that she was on a different plain to all of them.
Something had happened in there. Something which
she couldn't even begin to make sense of. But she
knew that every word that she heard was true. And
from this other place she wanted to shout to them,
"Hurry home, you poor fools. Go on; to your tellys
and your videos. You gowks!"

And the anger, intermingled with a devastating
pity, threatened to blind her. For she knew that they

were all there. Jimmy Mackay with his big expensive car that bespoke his expensive lifestyle. And Murdo Ferguson, who behind his so-respectable front had an over-fondness for young lassies. And what about you, lady of the manor? With all your fancy outfits and hats the size of a satellite dish. Ay, I bet that one you've on tonight could feed a fair number of poor bairns. You were all there!

And she felt it rising up in her.. And she was sore afraid.
"I saw you," her mind screamed. "How couldn't you see me? You couldn't miss me! Didn't you notice the supporting player? That was me! I hammered in the nails...
Oh Christ!"

AT THE TATTIES

With your tea in a large lemonade bottle and your sandwiches of margarine and jam wrapped up in a loaf paper you hurried out of the house at seven o'clock in the morning to catch the bogey at the corner. The excitement was great, you barely slept the night before for fear of sleeping in and missing the whole thing. Warmly wrapped up in your coat, pixie and rubber boots against the harsh October cold, you hardly took the time to say 'Cheerio' to your mother and father as you dashed from them, the only thing in your mind the securing of a good place in the trailer.

The wifies were there first, taking the best places around the sides, the boards to their backs, ensuring a fairly comfortable ride. Yourself and your small brother ended up in the centre, bedding down in the straw like a couple of hens. You were glad you had your coat. You snuggled your neck down into it as the frosty morning air sent the shivers all about you. Your feet were already losing the warmth that they took with them from the house, your exposed hands were freezing.

"Coorie doon in the straw," the wifies would tell you. And they'd make a bed for you. "Look, like that. Build the straw about yourselves and keep warm. That's the way."

You could climb into the bogey no bother at all. You were little and slamp. Some of the wifies were quite slamp too. Others, especially the fatter ones, couldn't hardly get in at all. Then those who were already there would shout to the mannie driving the tractor that this one was needing a leg up.

They climbed up at the trailer wheel and swung first one leg, then the other, over the side, tumbling into the straw inside. The first ones in helped the rest, especially the older or the heavier ones.

Big Bessie was the fattest. She was likely the fattest person that you ever knew. She'd get stuck at the wheel and laugh at it in her breathless voice, "Come leg, or I'll leave you." Then all the other wifies would laugh and make a joke with her as they tried to haul her hefty body on board; she'd nearly land on top of you and your small brother and you were very frightened. She was so big, with large legs as she wobbled near you, blocking out the morning.

Finally the tractorman would take his watch from his pocket and decide that it was time to be off.

"Are you all there?" he'd call out.

"If we were all there, we wouldna be here," Isa would call back, full of cheer and good fun even at that early hour.

"Right, if everyone's here, we're off," and he would

climb up into the tractor and start it. At the sound of the engine you felt afraid. It was very loud and sent your small brother tight against you. You looked at the wifies. They were all laughing and joking and you weren't worried anymore.

You rattled along, like Smarties in a tube, quiet in your excitement and incomprehension. The village was empty. You had never seen it like that, in the early morning darkness.

You didn't know where you were going and relied on the wifies, they knew everything. They had been lifting the tatties for years. When they started to get their bags together you knew that you must be coming to the field. Then you were there.

You had never seen anything like the field, it was large and flat and brown. The biggest thing you had ever seen before was the sea. You were used to the vastness of that, but the field was not like the sea, which moved, the tides coming in and out, sometimes throwing treasure onto the shore for you to find. You knew the sea and the rocks. You were always about them, but you weren't sure about the field. It just lay there, still and strange. It looked as big as the world. It would have plenty tatties.

The wifies tumbled from the bogey easier but slower than they had climbed in. Your small brother was the first off, jumping down by himself, not wanting anybody's help. You wouldn't show off like that. You let the tractorman give you a big lift down. He clapped your head and said you were a good lassie.

There were lots of cane baskets scattered the length of the field and immediately the old hands flew to the good new ones. Not knowing what to do, you just stood where you were and looked all about. You got the old broken hampers that were left, until Isa spotted the pair of you and put things right.

"That's no use to you. Here maital," and she'd hand you one of her new hampers and one which was quite decent. "And watch them," she'd add, "that Bessie'll have them off you as soon as look at you." Isa was good and kind to you and you felt safer with her because she was there.

The squad filtered along the length of the drill. Then the howls of protest began. The grieve was measuring the drill into stages and marking them off with a stick which he pushed into the ground. You liked the grieve, for he always smiled at you and knew your name.

"Ow vow! Will you look at the size of thon," howled Doll in protest, scattering the seagulls, "We'll all be dead!" Katac took up the clarion call: "Beel, Beel, what size of a stage is that? I'll no live."

The grieve took not the slightest notice of this annual howling match. His large tackety boots never broke stride as he continued with his measuring and Katac pursuing him:

"Ow vow Beel! Are you telling me that stage you're giving me is right? It's twice as big as the rest."

Anna Mac ran to her place at the start of the drill, her four new hampers and her piece bag bumping against her short body. She always had the first stage and as the digger ate into the field her length became shorter.

Katac could pick tatties with one hand. She was very fast, scooping them into the basket, and seemed to be finished before those beside her had hardly begun, the earth-caked fingers of her gloves slapping the ground.

Yourself and your small brother were taking a stage between you. The grieve pretended that he didn't believe you. "Gosh, bless me!" he said in his smiley way. You were six then and your brother five. The wind made his pale eyes water but he was quick

and would pick every single tattie that was turned up,
even the little tiny ones. He wouldn't miss any. He'd
run about all over tidying up. Sometimes he would
even clean up other people's. You wouldn't do that.
You would put them under your heel or kick ground
over them when you thought no-one was looking.
The two of you would run after the digger, stumbling
in the clayey earth, and hold out your hamper, receiv-
ing more ground and stones than tatties. You didn't
care what you got, didn't tire of this ploy, for you
knew that in one quick minute you would get your
baskets filled and then you wouldn't have to gather
your stage. Isa used to tell you to watch or you would
hurt yourselves. Once, the tractorman told your small
brother that he would tell your father, that soon
made you stop.

When you were too cold to pick fast, Isa would
help.

"Just you two start at the other end and we'll work
to meet in the middle," she'd say in her strong warm
way.

Big Bessie to the other side, was another story
altogether; you were a little bit wary of her, ever since
she near flattened you in the bogey. She was very
large, that was true, but what divided her from you
was that she didn't know how to be about children.
She never had any about her. She would tell you that
your eyesight was wrong and that if you thought that
that was where your stage ended, you had better look
again; for that was your tatties lying there, nobody
else's, and you had better get them lifted before the
gaffer came. Then your small brother would scurry
to do her bidding. Sometimes too, she would tell you
stories to make you frightened:

"Come now the pair of you. Be good bairns to
Bessie and I'll tell you a story," and she'd proceed in
her awful voice, *"The wind and the rain/ Sent ma*

daddy home again/ Go away from the window/ Bogey man..." and she'd laugh at you, as your small brother sat whimpering on his hamper that he was wanting his Da and Ma. "Now watch where I'm marking! That's the stickie there," she'd say, marking out a line well into her stage with the heel of her boot. In the beginning you did whatever she said, but then Isa, going right up to her, started on her:

"You Bessie! That's your tatties, no the bairns. Don't come with your tips here – if we all pick our own, everything will be alright," and she would walk past you muttering about people that were too lazy to get off their fat backsides. Isa was only a little wifie, but tough.

At half-yoking time your tea would only be warm, but some kind wifie would pour you some hot from her flask and give you a scone or a small cake, which you would not like to accept, being shy, though your stomach overcame you and you'd enjoy the food and the shared friendliness of the squad. Your small brother wouldn't look at anybody when eating, not even the wifie who was kind to him, but you knew that he was pleased, for he'd sit on the upturned hamper, kicking at the earth with the toe of his boot, his head bent into his chest.

After tea, like the others, you hurried to fill your bag with tatties to take home. Isa ensured that you picked good sized ones and that you filled it to the top. Some had large bags and they had to be well hidden from the grieve under the straw in the trailer, with a scatter of coats over them. Then they would go and pee behind the trailer or across the field behind a bush if there was one. You wouldn't pee in the field for anything. You'd rather burst to death before you did *that* in front of people. Everyone knew what you were crossing the field for. The wifies would make jokes of it but you got all hot inside thinking about it. Sometimes your small brother cried because he needed, or else because he wanted to go home or was cold, and you would have to sort him and tell him everything would be alright.

As the day wore on towards dinner time, the wifies' protest at this form of slave labour became more vociferous. The digger driver was the first to get it:

"Slow down," they'd shout as one, "we're no getting the time to straighten our backs." Then they'd grumble among themselves, "what we're needing to do is find a big stone and stick it in the next drill – that'd sort him and his digger!"

Then the grieve got it:

"Beel!" And, rising to crescendo the full length of the field, "Beel! Can you tell that fellow to go a wee bit slower. Ow vow – I'm near dead with him!" The grieve just smiled and said nothing, but went on shifting the marker sticks away from the encroaching machine. In the end the mannie emptying the hampers got it:

"That fellow's killing us – killing us all – we'd have been better going to Tulloch's," they'd peck, mentioning the name of the neighbouring farm.

When the digger stopped at the bottom of the drill bang on the dot of twelve, the stages were picked clean in record time. On seeing the others running for the bogey, your small brother would take off after them, leaving you to gather on your own, and you'd nearly rip your throat out shouting him back to do his share, but he wouldn't even turn around as he went straight to the trailer to get a good seat.

There was much pushing and shoving there, not all good natured, for the reserved places. At Big Bessie's request to your brother to move from *her* place Isa would give it to her: "There's no booked places in this bogey. Let the bairns be!"

You sat on your bag of tatties for the ride home, looking over the side of the trailer, watching the road going fast. Some of the wifies sang *'Show me the way to go home'*. Some were just tired. You could only hang there, smelling of the field, with your brother all groundy too, seated in Big Bessie's place.

The tractorman lifted your bag of tatties down for you and said that that was right good ones that you had there. You both climbed down by yourselves and you told your small brother that he had to take the other handle of the bag.

As you were going along the road you saw your father coming to meet you. He took the bag from you and said, "That's you. Your mother has the dinner all ready."

Your small brother said that he was doing his pee and that he wasn't going back. You held on to yourself and said nothing. You reached for you father's hand and went home.

T O   T H E M
T H A T   H A T H

Carefully, John placed the last lump of coal on the
fire. It huddled against the smouldering log, seeking
its warmth. When she had gone he would build the
dross over it and it would last for the rest of his day.
After supper he would go to bed, glad to lie down...

He drew his chair back in, hard against the tiles,
and stretching forward, his boney hands reached out
like sensors, seeking the heat. He rubbed them together, generating warmth, then bent forward once
more.

The girl was nice enough. Only a lassie really. The
Social Services had sent her out to assess his needs.
The home help had phoned them to see if he was
entitled to a hoover. Said the brush made the going

heavy on her.

Young or not, the girl was smart. As smart as new paint. And she had all the facts and figures at her bright pink finger tips. About the benefits that he might be able to get now that his health was going on him.

John looked at the girl, saw her mouth saying the words. He'd been going to the sea for years by the time he was that lassie's age. He left his home in this very village when he was just sixteen. Forty-eight years he'd been at sea. Coastal to begin with and then he went deep sea.

Valparaiso and Curacao! The names, the places, long lost in the mists of time came back in on him, enshrouding him in memory. He remembered the first time that he saw a black man. That was in Liverpool. And now he always associated brown shiny shoes and gold teeth with the black people.

The girl's insistent voice, close to his ear, drew him back into the present. He might be getting on but he wasn't deaf. His canary was beginning to kick up a fuss at the intrusive sound. What's that she was saying? Could he comb his own hair? John permitted himself a small, secret smile. Not much of his curls left now. And did he need help to get dressed or to go to the toilet? No? How was he during the night. Any problem with soiling then? No, nothing like that. He was still pretty good there. It was his legs. They were done. He always used to enjoy his walk to the pub. The walk was as good as the time spent there with his pint. But the pub was a mile away in the next village. A long way.

He was alright in the house. He could manage there. And he shaved himself every Tuesday and Saturday. And on Saturday's he'd change his under clothes. Oh, he was alright there. The home help did his bedding and that, but he saw to his own things.

He'd soak them in the pail in the Parozone and they came up like snow. He could see from the girl's face that she found this sort of thing distasteful. New at it, John expected. She said that it didn't leave him much dignity. Well that too went a long, long time ago.

His mind went back again. He was born when the First War ended. By the time he was twenty-one the Second War had begun. He was in the convoys then. They told him that he was a man and that his country needed him. And when that one was over, Labour were promising a land fit for heroes. So he voted for them. Not that he believed them. He wasn't that daft. Not for long, anyway. With the Welfare State he told himself that he'd seen the last of the poverty that he'd known as a boy. Then came the fifties and Harold MacMillan telling everyone they had never had it so good. And they hadn't – for a while anyway. They had moved from the old half-house into a new council house. The size of it put the bairns wrong, running about through all the rooms, turning on the taps as hard as they would go and pulling the plug in the lavatory. But he was getting on now and on his own; his family scattered far away from him.

The girl was at him again. She'd read in a paper about this professor fellow somewhere down in England. He had the notion that some foods lost their nutritional value when cooked. They were much better for you if consumed raw. That way he could save on electricity.

John looked sharply at the girl. Was she right? She was making a joke on him, surely. But no, she was being serious about it. Trying to cheer him up, she said that maybe the Chancellor would surprise him. Maybe there'd be something in it for the old people this time. John doubted it. He'd long lost respect for politicians of any colour or creed. There was nothing

to choose between them. He'd learnt that long ago.
Mouths full of promises they had no intention of
fulfilling. Out for what they could get, the lot of
them. Playing with people's lives.

After she had gone, John reached for his Bible.
He'd just hold it for a while. His was a generation that
knew its Bible, sought and found comfort in it. As his
thumb rubbed the smooth cover he thought of St
Matthew's Gospel. The bit about them that had, re-
ceiving, and them that had little or less having it taken
away from them.

With the winter dark coming and his coal done,
John thought of his £40 a week. The small remuner-
ation that he received from the Navy he never
touched. That was to bury him decent.

He thought of all the people in the world who were
in a much worse state than he was. The peoples in all
the places he'd been. And he thought about the bit
where The Lord had said to the people that when he
was hungry they didn't feed him and when he was
thirsty they didn't give him a drink, right down to the
bit where he was in prison and no-one visited him.
And the frightened people said, When Lord? When
didn't we do all these things? And the answer The
Lord gave – John could still remember His exact
words: "Verily, I say unto you, in as much as ye did it
not unto the least of these my brethren, ye have done
it not unto me!"   And John thought that if Matthew
had the right of it, it was hard to see where any of
them that were running the world were heading,
except straight for Hell itself.

The coal had settled to a red glow. John shovelled
the dross over it, banking it up at the back. He should
have offered the girl a cup of tea. She was a nice girl.
He would have, but he only had enough milk left for
the porridge which he would take for his supper.

OLD JOHNDY & LITTLE JOHN

One day when old Johndy was walking up from the harbour he saw little John coming along the shore, his eyes at his feet to see what he could find. He laid aside the damaged creel that he was carrying and hailed the little fellow.

"What now my brochach?" he called, his hand raised in greeting, and as the boy drew abreast of him, "What are you saying to it then?"

"Ay ay John," returned the bairn, giving him his right name.

"And where were you at the day?"

"Over at the bay," the small fellow replied.

"Well it's a nice enough day to be over there. Did you go into the water?" Johndy asked, knowing well that he must have, for his hair was clapped flat to his head.

"Me and Davie were in for a wee while. It's cold though. Then we were jumping the channel. I'm nearly getting as good as Davie."

The channel was a deep gouge in the rocks. It was about ten feet deep and four feet across, a mighty distance for short legs. Add to that the surface from which you had to take off and land, plus the added danger of the depth of water when the tide was coming in, and the fear that gripped the breast of mothers who knew what their bairns were at was all too understandable.

"You better watch yourself from that channel now. If you were to fall and the tide coming, it would be the end of you. Now listen to what I'm saying to you." The old man was serious in his warning. The boy looked up at him with pale blue eyes as he continued, "Always mind yourself from the rocks. What would your mother do if anything was to happen to you?"

The boy said nothing. He turned from old Johndy and began kicking at the sand with the toe of his left sandal.

"Well now," said the seaman to the bent head, "Do you know what I saw when I was lifting the clighs?" and there was a warm glint, deep in the brown eyes that addressed the child.

"What?" said little John grudgingly.

"Seals. What do you say to that?"

"Seals?" repeated little John giving the old man all of his attention.

"Down yonder," and Johndy lifted his arm and pointed to the east. "Down at the Point. Three of them. Two big ones and a little young one. And they weren't afraid. Came right up to the boat. I could've touched them. The wee one was just like a Labrador puppy."

"Did you touch them?"

"No, I didn't do that. I just sat down in the boat and looked at them."

"I wish I could've seen them. I would just look at

them too. I wouldn't frighten them."

"And maybe you will one day, my boy. I know that they would like to see you."

"Do you think they would?"

"Surely."

Sometimes little John's father would take him to the lobsters. At such times he would be unable to sleep the night before, such was the excitement that was in him. This brought the remonstrance from his mother that people who got no sleep needn't expect to be on the sea in the morning. Then little John would throw himself on to the pillow and with loud deep breaths show her how hard he was sleeping – like a rock. In the beginning, when he couldn't control the feeling that was going on in him he'd count the small black dots that were clustered around the autumn leaves on the wallpaper. But the feeling would prove too much for him and although he counted every dot in the room a dozen times he would still be wide awake. Then in the morning his father would come and shake him and ask was he fit and tell him that his mother had the porridge waiting on him.

The times on the sea with his father were the best times. More than once they were close to the dolphins that swam about in the firth. The old ones called them the paillacs. He'd seen them many times from the shore, through his father's glasses. Out beside them they were huge, leaping from the water and crashing down heavily, nearly swamping the boat. Little John thought that they were the bonniest things that he had ever seen. The seals would be bonny too, but he had only ever seen one of them lying dead on the shore; he didn't look at it as he hurried past, holding his nose from the smell.

"Are you wanting to see my stone?" he now asked

Johndy.

"And what stone is that?"

Little John took the small round smooth pebble from his trouser pocket and handed it to old Johndy. The old man studied the stone quietly. Then he weighed it in his right hand. Finally he held it up to the light and looked at the sky behind it. Wordlessly he handed it back to little John, a thoughtful look on the old lined face.

"Oh, valakan," he said at length. "Where did you find it?"

"Out at the white rock. Me and Davie were looking for juntachs in the well."

"Show it to me again."

Little John handed him the stone and he looked closely at it once more. He was thinking it must be the same stone. That shape, the colours, the hole in the centre. The only other one that he had ever seen like it was the one he himself found when he was about this bairn's age. This stone was smoother, he'd grant that. But time and tides would see to that. The same black and pink marbling running through it. But it was more than that. He just had to hold it to know. He'd been about the shore all his life and he'd never seen another. Till now.

Little John was becoming impatient with his friend. What did he take his stone again for? And just sitting there on the harbour looking at it, saying nothing.

"It's a good stone, eh?" he blurted out, unable to hold himself any longer.

"Oh, it's more than that," the old fellow said queerly. "It's more than that. If I'm not mistaken it's a very special stone you have there."

"What way is it special?"

Old Johndy sat there looking at the boy silently, then he reached forward his hand to him.

"Jump up here now and listen to what I'm going to

tell you."

Little John climbed up on the harbour to sit beside
old Johndy, legs stretched straight before him and
looked to where the salt water had left a white wave
on his sandals. One look, and his mother would know
that he had been on the rocks; she was apt to overdo
things then. Sometimes she'd still be speaking about
the price of shoes – and where did he think they were
coming from and how that Davie would land him in
trouble one day – when he was taking his supper, and
his father would hear.

He moved in beside old Johndy and gave him all of
his attention.

The old man folded his arms across his breast,
crossed his legs at the ankles, took a deep breath and
began his story.

"Well now. One day, I'm minding I would have
been about your own age, ten is it?" and he inclined
his head to little John for confirmation.

"I'm nearly ten," little John jumped in helpfully.

"That's right. Well, as I was saying, I was ten and in
that days we were never off the shore. And in the
summer holidays we practically lived on it. And do
you know what we were doing?" And again he looked
to the little fellow, who shook his head in reply.

"The same as yourself was doing before you came –
jumping the channel. My granny used to give it to me
when she found out. There was a whole crowd of us
and some had made boats from the corks off the nets.
Oh, the laughs that was in it, racing the boats. *Come
on the Maid*. We gave them names you know. Mine
was *The Maid of Morveth*. That was my grandfather's boat. A big boat. Well, there we were. Nearly
falling into the water with the laughing that was on us
at Ake Tarrel. His boat was going round in circles.
And then Ake shouts 'Look at mine, boys. Look how

she's going.' Look at where she's going more like.
Backwards. Ach, she was too light."

Little John liked old Johndy's stories but as he
shifted himself on the stony surface he wished that he
would tell him. He would have to be going soon.
Then there was the business of trying to dodge past
his mother without her seeing the state of his feet.

The old man picked up again. "Well, as you yourself know, when it's the holidays and you're on the
shore, there's no word of dinners or work waiting on
you or anything. There's other things to be doing.
Well that was the way it was with us. Skylarking. The
way boys are."

"But what about my stone?" little John pressed.

"Am I no coming to that," said old Johndy who
would not shift from first gear. "Well, here's me, the
best channel jumper that was ever in it. I could land,
oh ten feet easily on the other side. Well that's what
we were at. Then I saw my granny coming to get me.
I was always remembering that I had to go to the well,
but I was trying hard not to, if you grasp my meaning."

Little John nodded that he did.

"Well, she couldn't wait any longer. Did I think that
clothes washed themselves? They were my clothes,
not hers. She couldn't keep clean clothes to me in the
holidays. And the hens might die of thirst for all that
I would care. Oh, she didn't half give it to me. Maybe
I was expecting an old woman like herself to lift the
water, and her with a big lad in the house."   Old
Johndy looked at little John, saw the lips part, ready
to speak and said quickly.

"I know what you're thinking. Well I came. She was
right enough and she was only a little woman and old
you know. Now, when you're walking on the shore
your eyes are always at your feet. Am I right?"

"You're right."

"Now, just as I drew level with the white rock, my eyes were right where they were right to be, and there I found it. The stone I'm telling you about."

Little John was about to say something but he held his peace and old Johndy proceeded. "I had never seen the like of it in my life. And no-one I showed it to did either."

"And what was your stone like?"

"Gosh bless me boy, is that no what I'm telling you." He jabbed his long boney fore-finger at little John's hand. "That stone. That stone there in your hand."

"How do you know it's the same one?"

"It's the same alright."

"Are you sure?"

"As sure as I am that you're sitting beside me right now. My granny didn't like the look of it. When I showed it to her she cried something in the Gaelic that I didn't understand. She was always going off like that when she was troubled. She told me to throw it from me, as far as my arm could drive."

"And did you?"

"Indeed I did not. I went against her there, for I had never seen such a lovely stone. It's a bit worn now. No, I only laughed at her. That's the way of it when you're young, my boy. You think you are the very first generation in the entire history of the world that knows things."

"Is that your story?" Little John was disdainful in his disappointment. "Your granny frightened of a stone. My granny wouldn't be frightened. She wouldn't be frightened of anything."

"No I don't believe she would," said old Johndy. "But these were different times. Now then," and little John settled himself and waited to hear the rest of the story.

"Well, I was coming home from the bay one day as

usual. This would be, oh maybe two years later."

"That's when you would be twelve."

"You're right. You can do your sums. I was twelve then," he confided to little John, his left hand going up to scratch behind his ear. "I was coming to the white rock again. The tide was out so you could see the rock. I was looking up into the sky through the hole in the stone. There was one or two puffball clouds I seem to remember. And just as I came to the rock, everything about me turned to gold. The rocks were all golden, the sea far out was rippling gold. I was standing up to my ankles on sand like gold dust."

"Was yourself gold?" breathed little John as the spell bound him.

"Do you know I couldn't tell you. I never got the time to look. But the most startling thing of all was the white rock. Sitting on it, and remember all the rocks were golden, sitting on it – was a mermaid."

"A mermaid," repeated little John, his breath almost stopping on him.

"I'll never forget what I saw," said the old man, "The loveliest creature surely that ever the world could hold. She was sitting on the white rock combing her hair. It was golden and reached right down her back."

"Did she speak to you?"

"No, maital. She was singing. The sweetest sound you ever heard. I think maybe that mermaids must be sisters to the angels."

"Well, did you say anything to her?" Little John was gripped with a desperate urgency.

"No. No. It was just a split second thing you see. Gone by the time I blinked my eye. I looked, and when I started to breath again it was all gone. Just like it had never happened. Afterwards the shore was a dull dark place to be. I felt the cold come into me. Even the white rock was black then. I kept looking for her but I never saw her again. Then I lost the stone. Through a hole in my pocket."

"Did you tell anyone what you saw?"

"No, I never did."

"Were you frightened that they wouldn't believe you or maybe they would laugh at you?"

"Indeed and I know they would. For I was not the first in these parts to see one. When I was little I grew up with the story of Hughie Vorran. I never knew him. He was dead by then. But when Hughie was young he saw the mermaid and he told anyone that he could get hold of. He couldn't get over what he had seen do you see?"

"And did they laugh at him?"

"They did. He died an old man and even after he was dead they were still talking about him. Ach," old Johndy waved his hand aside, "He wouldn't let folk be, so in the end whenever they saw him coming they would cut down vennels or go along the shore so that they would miss him. Either that or they would get him to tell them again so that they could have a laugh against him."

Old Johndy was quiet for a short time, then he looked at the boy. "So I never said a word to a soul. Till now. Yourself is the first that knows."

"I'll never tell anyone in my whole life," promised little John, looking straight into the old man's eyes. "Honest to God."

Old Johndy smiled at the small boy, said nothing, then clapped his hand to the fair hair, made coarse by the salty water.

"Well," he said, rousing himself, "It's time we were some place else. There'll be meat waiting on the pair of us. Catch an end of that cligh."

The little fellow gripped one end of the lobster pot, the old cawnhar the other and together they crossed the shingle to the bank.

"We'll just leave it here with the rest for now," said old Johndy as he let go his end beside the cluster of pots needing repair which were already there.

The boy spoke and it seemed as if something heavy in him was being eased away.

"John, do you think my stone is magic?" he whispered.

Johndy straightened his back and looked out to the sea.

"Well, I have often thought of it and the answer's no. My granny had no need to be frightened. But as I said, these were different times. No, your stone is just that. A bonnie stone I'll grant you. That's why seeing your stone startled me. It brought back on me what happened to myself. No John, maital, I believe that the magic is in the people"

"Is it in everybody?"

"Surely. You just have to recognize it's there."

"Is it in me?"

"Oh I would say that it would be. Yes, a boy like yourself would have it in him alright. Mind you," old Johndy chuckled, "I'm no saying that you'll see a mermaid. One day you might see the seals though. We'll have to see."

Little John was feeling new as he walked towards his home. Old Johndy thought that he had magic in him. It would be true. Old Johndy knew an awful lot of things. He probably knew nearly as much as his own father.

His attention was drawn to his feet as they slapped the road. The tide marks were becoming more pronounced as they dried out. Soon they'd be up to his ankles. He wondered if he could magic things away. He took the stone from his pocket and held it up to the sky.

L O V E   S T O R Y

As Donald took his supper of fish soup he was aware,
behind the noise of the storm, of the quiet contented
sound of his mother's humming as she busied herself
about the fireplace, adding more wood to the fire,
pouring the boiling water on to the leaves in the pot.

This past year she appeared to him more like the
mother that dwelt far back in his memory. From
somewhere a long way off he had this in him of a
smiling face, crooning to him when he could not
sleep, frightened by the wind which howled about
their house and the noise of the breakers pounding
the shore, like to smash the rocks to smithereens. In
the difficult times he had tried hard to hold fast to
this memory, and to that other of his girl- mother,

racing with him along the shore as they searched for
driftwood or coal from a wrecked vessel, her laughter
rising and falling like the swell on the sea, or stopping
the seagulls in their crying. And, hard on its heels
came the one of a young man, not much older than
himself; this man was dark haired, (unlike himself
who had the very fair colouring of his mother's
people), a tall man, hardy he now knew, with black
eyes that looked on the world as if it were a huge joke.
This memory Donald could hardly bear to examine
and so for the past six years he turned his back on it
and closed that particular door.

For Donald's father had been one of the Hilltown
men who went to the aid of *The Linnet Mhor*, when
she ran aground out in the firth. That they had
managed to get the whole crew ashore was brave; but
in lightening the ship so as to be able to sail her into
port for repairs, it was believed they over-did it and
the gale drove the ship onto the rocks and every man
was drowned.

This had deranged his mother. For weeks afterwards she combed the shore, unwilling to believe that
her man had gone from her. The women did their
best to dissuade her, pointing out the impossibility of
anyone surviving in such mountainous seas, for none
of the men could swim.

She'd take Donald with her and frantically bid him
to search behind this rock and that one, while she in
her madness would wade out into the sea crying for
her Domhnull to come to her.

At last she resigned herself to the fact that he
would not return from the sea. She then entered a
world where no human lived; still going about her
work, bent keening and wailing to the washing or
baking. And still she went to the shore, returning with
her bundle of driftwood and with something resembling peace on her features. Most days Donald

went with her, the fear thumping at his breast whenever she went from his sight in case she would do anything on herself. For now she never loitered about the shore as she used to, showing him the different shells and pointing out to him the differing colours and shapes of the stones there. Instead she took off at a running walk as if she were desperate to get some place. And there were times when she sat down on the bank or on a rock and seemed to forget where she was. She would have sat there interminably with him gently beseeching her that it was time for them to return, that the dark would soon be on them. Then she'd look up at him with eyes that were flat and dead. She'd rise from her place and gently he'd guide her home.

In the beginning, she refused to go the bed she had shared with his father. For a long time she refused. When he went ben to the box-bed in the closet she'd sit on the small stool that his father had made for him and stare into the dying embers of the fire, as if to find there an answer to the question her mind didn't know how to ask. He'd urge her to her bed from the cold but she would repel him. In the end he didn't try to press her but when it was time to go through, he'd fetch her her warm woollen shawl. Once she told Donald that she had knitted it when she was just his age for her own mother, now dead. She died in the glen the year that they cleared the people from their houses and from their land. And it was after that that his father and herself came to live down here by the shore, to try to make their living from the fishing. His grandfather had come with them but he did not last long in the new place. And then little Donald had arrived. That was the best day that was ever in it for herself and his father.

Donald had heard the stories of the hardships they faced, both in the glen and in the new place, but the

hardest thing of all to bear was the thought of those
who no longer dwelt among them. Whether they
went to Canada or Glasgow or just further down the
coast mattered little. They weren't with them and
their hearts were sore and doubly sore, for they also
felt acutely the pain of their friends and families
missing them.

Donald pushed the bowl from him and, scraping
his chair back, got to his feet. He reached for his
bonnet and went towards the door.

"I'll not be many minutes," he flung over his
shoulder to his mother. "That's a wild night that's in
it. I'm thinking to pull the boat up as far as the bank.
If not we could yet lose her," and he stepped into the
fierce, darkening night, the door slamming at his
back.

His mother rinsed the dishes in the bucket of water
and replaced them on the dresser. She was thinking
how bright the days seemed to her now. For a long,
long time she didn't believe she would see that bright-
ness anywhere or in anything again. She picked up
the geansaidh she was knitting for Donald and drew
her chair into the fire. The light from the lamp threw
shadows onto the walls of the room, making it appear
that other people dwelt there. Outside the storm
raged. Once it had raged like that within herself. The
loud ticking of the clock, the rhythmic clicking of the
needles were as balm to the heart of the woman by the
fireside. Her thought was on Donald, as it always was.
In their role reversal, he but a child had to become a
man, while she became the helpless, the dependant
one. At twelve years of age he had to assume the
mantle that his father had never had, for his father
did not have to watch out for someone with no sense
of their own. And she thought not only of her own
son but of all the boys whose fathers went down on

The Linnet Mhor.

Two years later Donald got a place on Hector Ross's boat and did the work of a man. In her anxious state she showed her fear of the sea to him. Angrily and defiantly he had resisted her, cruelly laughing at her as he tore himself from the fingers that clawed, and tried so hard to hold him. She knew that she would see for the rest of her life the tears in the eyes of her son that first time he went through the door – the boy who was trying so hard to be a man.

For Donald was of the new generation who grew up in the village and expected to live by the sea. In that respect he was at one with the boys whose forebears came from these parts and to whom the sea called from the time that they could walk. Donald knew nothing of what it was like to live in the glen and so could not be torn between the old ways and these ways; he had been born in a stone house built by the shore in this very fishertown. He was a dooan – a Hilltown fisher. The sea, in all its moods coursed through his veins, his heart beat to its rhythms and not to the rythms of the earth, as her own and his father's had and their people before them. And now at twenty years of age he had his own boat and crew.

She knew that she would never rid herself of her fear of the sea; that hungry sea, voracious and insatiable. She wouldn't think of those who had succumbed to its gaping mouth in their first years; this alien element. She had come to terms with her fear however. That was the good thing to come from Domhnull's death. It forced her to take her fear, largely born from ignorance, and to look at it; for the first time to understand it, and in that understanding the fear itself abated somewhat, became somehow a reasoned thing. And with that had come another lightening of spirit, so that she felt twice re-awakened. She did not seek this, had never thought to look for it, but in the dawning of her new day it had sought and found her.

Donald didn't know. She barely knew herself what it was. So sweet did it feel that she kept tasting it to make sure that it was real and not a ghost drifting by from the unreality of the past. Her step was light now and her eye quick as she went about her work, her head high and proud once more. And the singing was back in her heart... These things had been coming gradually as she mended, but the gleam that was on her didn't come from there. It came from some place else and warmed her right through to the soul.

The light from the lamp turned her hair to the colour of the corn and softened the gentle features still more; so that they were of the girl she had been before sorrows touched her. The knitting needles beat out their quiet rhythm keeping time with the ticking of the clock.

As soon as he put his face outside, Donald felt the hail-stones sting his face. Hastily he closed the door, turned up the collar of his jacket, thrust his hands deep into his pockets and bent his head to the wind. Farther along the row he came to Hugh Vass's father's house. He rapped on the door. Hugh was one of his crew, also twenty years of age. Hugh himself answered the knock and on seeing Donald standing there immediately followed. No words were used or needed.

Some of the other crews had already hauled their boats above the high water mark, some were in the act of performing this operation and the remainder were making their way down along with Donald and Hugh. The men acknowledged each other by a raised hand; any words would have been torn from them by the gale or lost in the roar from the sea.

When they had pushed their boat up a few feet,

Hugh ran to grasp the rollers, placing them below the forward part of the boat. Once more the men heaved.

"Come on Hugh man. Exert yourself!" yelled Donald into the teeth of the gale.

They repeated the process with the rollers a few times and finally had the boat well up. In the worst storms, the sea washed up over the bank and on one occasion had actually entered the houses; although it was angry tonight, that did not look like happening.

Donald and Hugh called goodnight to the men still on the shore, climbed the bank and walked to their homes.

It was as he was passing the vennel between old Morag's house and Artair Morrison the shopkeeper's, that a small figure hurtled into him as if it had been tossed there by the wind. Her head, which was covered in a shawl was bent into her chest, obliterating her vision. Donald reached forward a steadying hand and felt rather than heard the indrawn breath.

"Where's the fire then?" he said awkwardly, drawing his hand back.

"Oh, it's you Donald Mackay," said Margaret Morrison, lifting her head and looking up at him.

"It is. Myself and Hugh were down at the boat. It's a wild enough night anyway."

Donald always felt himself complicated whenever he was in Margaret Morrison's company. It wasn't so bad if a few of them were together, at the ceilidhs or gathering the whelks. He could be quite forward then and would give every bit as good as he got and didn't lag behind with the quick joke. To be alone with her however, was another story altogether; he tied himself into all kinds of knots and if it wasn't for the darkening night he knew that she would now take endless pleasure from the dark flush he knew was spreading from his throat.

"I'm just back from Ishbel and Ian's. It won't be

long now until Ishbel has her baby. Everyone's been so kind. Do you know, she got four shawls," the girl's light laughter pierced him.

"That's very good. Ishbel will be pleased enough about that. Poor Ian. Soon there'll be no sleep in it for him."

"Oh you! What a thing to say. It may interest you to know that Ian's more impatient than Ishbel for this baby." At the unyielding expression on the face above her she went on, "Anyway, how's your mother? I'm sorry I've not been along to see her. Father's been keeping me at it in the shop. Will you tell her that I'm asking for her?" the girl said kindly as she drew her shawl tighter about her.

Donald looked down at this girl, who barely reached up to his oxter. So small and neat was she that one might wonder that she was able to keep her footing against such a strong wind. To think like that would be wrong, for as well as being blessed with good health she was as strong as a horse; as Donald could testify from their growing up days, when as children they ran and played together. There was no strangeness between them in those brother and sister days. Then it had begun to change; the playing stopped and the girls were given over to loud giggling from behind their hands and long, sidelong glances. Donald hadn't a notion what it was all about and missed the easy friendship that helped to make the time with his mother more bearable. Ian had got to grips with the new situation quickly enough; two years ago he married Ishbel and they went to live in his grandmother's house. Now they awaited the birth of their second child.

"My mother is very well," Donald answered. "And how is your father?"

"My father is fine. Although he is creating something awful about myself going away."

When he had recovered sufficiently Donald asked, "Away? Away where?" He could not imagine the village without that vital spark that was Margaret Morrison.

"Well if you must know I'm away to the herring, with Jessie. We'll travel to Helmsdale on Monday."

"Oh. That will be very fine for you." And unable to stop himself, "You'll likely meet someone there."

"Do you think so," she teased. "I expect I'll meet lots of nice people up there," and again he caught that laughter in her throat.

"Anyway, I'd best be getting back. My mother'll wonder what's keeping me," he added feebly.

"Well, goodbye Donald, and remember me to your mother," Margaret Morrison said as she moved away.

"Goodbye," said Donald. And unable to hold himself, "And be sure to watch yourself up there."

"I will," she called back. "Ta-ta." And then she was gone, her slight body curved to the gale, her skirts whipped around her ankles.

Donald's mother laid aside her knitting as he came in. When he had crossed the room she spoke.

"Did you manage to get the boat up?"

"We did."

She settled back to her knitting, for a short time nothing more was said.

"Did you hear Margaret Morrison is away to the herring on Monday? Up to Helmsdale," Donald blurted out as he sat down on the other side of the fireplace across from his mother.

She laid aside the geansaidh and looked on the troubled countenance of her son. Donald was young, but from that lost time he had emerged with a wisdom that years alone could not give. As the flames from the fire licked the fair curls to gold, her eyes caught the large, capable hands hanging loosely between his knees and her breath almost stopped in her breast. She knew better than he himself did how he felt about Margaret Morrison. And who wouldn't feel like that about her? As light and as quick as a flame. With the laughing brown eyes on her that any man would consider it an honour to drown in. And the dimples in her cheeks whenever she talked. As a child she was never far from Donald. Always Margaret and Donald it was and Ian and Ishbel. Well, Ian and Ishbel were married, and now Margaret was leaving the village and he did not know what way to think. "I heard from Belle Ross that she is to go with her, Jessie and the other girls. It'll be a good thing for them to see what it's like outside the village, although I think Margaret's father is afraid for her. He needn't be. He protects her too much. Margaret is a fine, good girl."

"You didn't think to tell me," he accused hotly, the heat from the fire adding to the angry colour on his face.

His mother said nothing.

Donald reached up and raked his right hand through his hair, then reached for the poker and drove it viciously into the heart of the fire, disturbing the embers.

"Well, putting the fire out on us is not going to alter matters. In truth I did not know what to say – I know how you feel about the girl."

Donald laid the poker down, saying nothing.

"She was going Donald, speaking was not going to change anything. Her father tried hard enough."

"In any case, what does it matter to me? She's free to go wherever she likes. She's nothing to me."

His mother kept her counsel and allowed him to empty himself. Anyone with half an eye could see what Margaret Morrison was to her son. But how could he take another woman to live in his mother's house. Two women sharing the one house. Never, in the days of creation had such a thing ever been heard of. And if he were to take a wife and find a home of their own, what then of herself? A widow could not manage on her own, she needed a man to provide for, in her case her only son. She knew the line of Donald's thinking. He would never leave her. What she wanted for him could not arise.

She searched around for the correct words as he sat there glowering at the kettle on the hook as if it had long since done some wicked thing on him. "I'm going to marry Artair Morrison, when the fishing season finishes," she dropped the words into the silence that hung between them.

When he didn't answer, she thought that he hadn't heard. Then, slowly he straightened his back, caught her eyes and held them.

"I knew nothing about this. Why didn't I know?"

"I did not know myself until Wednesday. Artair walked home with me from the meeting-house."

"Well, he always liked you well enough anyway. You'll be going to live in his house. Does Margaret know?"

"I don't think Margaret knows yet. But I wanted you to know how things are. It is right that you should know."

"I don't know what to say. There was always just you and myself."

"After your father died I would not be in it but for you, Donald. But you have your own life. It is right that you have it," and the eyes of blue looked deep into his own as she added shyly, "I'll be able to help Artair in the shop."

"Will you like that, do you think?"

"I think I shall. Oh, don't you see Donald, it's time for me to go on also. No more turning my head to the past."

Donald said nothing. His mother carried on.

"Donald, mo ghaoil," she used the old endearment, "Margaret will not be away for a long time. The herring season will pass soon enough and then she'll come home to us again. Then it will be up to you."

"I don't know what to say."

"I have taken your breath away from you. I can see that. But you have time, Donald. Time to get things straight. Margaret will come home, her father and myself will be married and yourself will have everything right again... Artair Morrison's a good man. I'm lucky that he will take me. Your father always had a good word for him."

"That's true. I have never heard anyone say worse than his name about him. But it's him that's the lucky one," the son in Donald railed.

"Anyway, I have told you. I'm glad I have, for I would not like for it to come between us. Now I'm away to my bed. You'll not be long if you're wise."

Donald sat on, oblivious to the storm outside and the fire dying on him. The reason for his mother's lightening of mood these past months was now plain to him. His mind groped around for all her news would mean. Margaret still liked him. At least he thought that she did. She was nice to him whenever he went into the shop. And she didn't seem to care for anyone else. That was always something. There were times, he had to admit, when she seemed to derive enjoyment from his discomfiture but that was nothing new; he grew up with her, he knew the way she was. Floating unbidden into his mind came a picture from the time when they were both about twelve. With Ishbel and Ian they were playing about in the sand dunes, trying to see who could jump the furthest, the soft sand made the landing easy. Margaret had tired of his boasting about his long jumps. To quieten him she

threw a large divot at the back of his head (another
thing about her was that her aim was true, as good as
any boy.) A furious wrestling match in the sand en-
sued with Ishbel and Ian cheering from the bank, as
Margaret wriggled beneath him like a lugworm. Even
yet he remembered the strength of her as knees,
elbows, and boots drove into every part of him.

He shook the memory from him and banked up the
fire. As he shovelled the fuel on, he thought that the
one good thing to come from a coal ship being
wrecked in the firth was the coal that was washed
ashore for long afterwards. It was a great joy and help
to the people of the village.

   This done, Donald went to the door for a last look
at the sky; then he killed the flame in the lamp and
went ben to his bed. The morning would come soon
enough.

PARTY PLAN

In the shop the day was early. The first rush of shoppers who came in for their morning rolls and papers was over. Now, at around eleven o'clock, things had settled and only the odd customer drifted in. It would be this way until about half past twelve when numbers would swell again as housewives hurried to catch the shop before closing time.

In this lull the two women were taking things easy. The younger, dark-haired girl had a woman's magazine spread open on the counter. From it she was reading the older woman's horoscope to her.

"Right Mina, are you listening? Friday – that's today – finds you working hard on your love life and on Saturday this takes a turn for the better."

The older woman was busying herself refilling the

shelves behind the counter with cigarettes, tobaccos, matches and the like. She stopped a moment and gave the girl her attention.

"What a lot of rot. Don't tell me you believe that stuff."

"Mina," gasped the young woman in mock indignation. "You've no romance in you. This could apply to you, you know," she teased.

"Ay, that'll be right," snorted the other. "I'll leave all that guff to you young ones. Believe me lassie, you're better off with a good cup of tea," and, trying not to smile she went back to her work.

"I know you, Mina – I bet yourself and Willie enjoy a wee cuddle still."

"I'm saying nothing," the other woman said, the corner of her eye catching the open door, "Anyway, you've a customer."

A poor-looking, thin woman had come into the shop. She had two children with her. One lay back in a pushchair, sucking at a bottle of tea, the slightly older one was holding fast to the handle of the pushchair.

"If she's wanting credit again she's going to be disappointed," the young woman said from beneath her breath. "You know what we were told the last time."

"Well," the older woman said, "just serve her and see what she wants."

"Och you do it, Mina. You're better at that sort of thing than me."

"I'm doing this. You go."

The young girl looked at the pale-faced woman in the fawn quilted coat.

"Could I have some things and I'll pay next Friday?"

"Sorry," said the girl in the overall, and she pointed to the notice pinned to the shelf where the cigarettes were. In large black letters it read 'NO CREDIT GIVEN' and was signed at the bottom with the proprietor's name, J. Patience.

"I'm sorry. We're not allowed to give credit. Mr Patience doesn't allow it."

"Just one or two things," she pleaded. "Please. I'll pay on Friday. I'll get the pay then."

The serving girl shook her head. She didn't like this sort of thing. She wished they wouldn't ask. "I'm sorry. We're not allowed."

"If I could just have some things for them," and she indicated the quiet children.

The girl was about to deny her a third time, when the older woman spoke.

"Look, dear, what is it you're wanting?"

Her colleague looked at her sharply and broke in.

"Mina," she hissed, "you know what Jack said. He's tired of being made a fool. You know what some of them up in the scheme are like. Here today then off and a string of unpaid bills left behind them."

"I know that fine," the older woman agreed. "But look at them. Look at that poor little things there." She took the young girl aside. "How many bairns that age do you know who never open their mouths in a shop? Usually they're all over the place, wanting this, wanting that, picking up everything that their little hands can lift and near dementing their mothers. That poor little things haven't the energy."

She turned back to the customer and said brightly once more, "Now, dear, what is it that you're needing?"

"Well, on your own head be it, that's all I'm saying," was the other's final word as she turned to refilling the shelves.

The customer took from her coat pocket a crumpled piece of paper on which she had written her needs. The older woman gathered together the goods and reached up to the top shelf, above the tobaccos for the bottle of vodka.

As she filled the plastic carrier bag she said, "Now, you'll pay next Friday."

The woman nodded.

"Then I'll no put it in the book. It'll just be between the two of us. I'll keep your slip," she said, folding the piece of paper and putting it in her overall pocket.

The woman and her silent children left the shop. The older assistant picked up a parcel of cigarettes, took two packets from it and needlessly added these to the full shelf. The young girl had helped herself to a chocolate bar. Peeling the silver paper from it she accused, "You've started something now. And giving her drink. You'll never get rid of her. She'll be back, just watch. You know what that lot are like."

The older woman ignored this and asked, "Do you know who she is?"

"Only for seeing. One of that ones up in the scheme."

"Is her man working?"

"As far as I know. I think they came up from Coatbridge or some place like that."

"Muir her name is. That's what she put on the paper."

She drew it from her pocket and studied it. " K. Muir. Is that a 'K' or an 'R' would you say?"

The girl looked at it and shook her head.

"I don't know. It could be either."

"Well, they were poor-enough looking things anyway."

"She looked as if a good feed might kill her," said the girl, pushing the chocolate into her mouth. "What are you going to do if she doesn't pay next Friday?"

"I'll sort that out when Friday comes," the older woman said. "And don't you say a word to anyone."

"It's nothing to do with me," the girl said and bent

over her magazine again. Winding a lock of her long curly hair around her right forefinger she murmured, "Know what it says for me? 'Venus is zapping you with romantic impulses. It's time to get smoochy with someone'. Mmm..."

The other shook her head and rolled her eyes up to heaven, saying nothing.

The following Friday the woman with the two shadowy children was true to her word. She paid the money she owed and asked if she could have some other things on credit. The next Tuesday she was back asking for more. It was alright, she would settle on Friday, her man came home on a Friday, with his pay. When she came in on the Thursday the young assistant could hold her tongue no longer.

"Mina, I hope you know what you're doing. I'm starting to get worried. She owes a fair amount."

"She promised she'd be in on Friday. I just have to trust her. There's not much else I can do."

The woman did come in and clear her debts. The older woman didn't say 'I told you so' to the younger girl, but her relief was evident.

The woman continued coming for the next few weeks. She was coming more often, but she always paid up on the Friday. Mr Patience didn't know, so there was no problem.

Yet the older woman was beginning to get uneasy. This thing she had begun looked as if it might get away on her. And she just didn't like giving the drink on tick. Necessities were one thing, and with bairns concerned what the eye didn't see the heart wasn't going to grieve over.

"Tell her!" the young one urged. "What's the point of worrying yourself. It's not your problem Mina."

"I think I'm going to have to. Once a week was alright but now there's a big lump of money lying out.

She was in three days last week and had a bottle of
vodka each day."
"I'm telling you. She found a soft mark in you,
Mina. Tell her when she comes in to pay. Explain that
it's worrying you. She'll have to like it or lump it,
that's all."
The older woman was too late. There was no sign
of her that Friday. The assistants waited until closing
time, but still she didn't come. The kind-hearted
woman had it on her mind the entire weekend. She
held fast to the hope that all would be right on the
Monday.
"What are you going to do?" the girl asked on the
Monday.
"What can I do?" replied the other. "Pay it myself.
There's nearly sixty pound lying out."
"That's a whole week's wages."
"I know that too. Well, maybe it will learn me."
The girl was sympathetic and hopeful. "She might
be in yet," she suggested.
The older woman shook her head. "You were
right," and she began weighing out potatoes and
putting them into plastic bags.
Just before dinner closing that day, Mrs Ivy
Bethune came bustling into the shop. With her she
had two little quiet children, both girls. One was lying
back in her pushchair, the other, with the long fair
hair, was gripping tight to the handle.
The two shop assistants looked at each other wordlessly. The young one spoke. "That's the little Muir
bairns. What's Mrs Bethune doing with them?"
Mrs Bethune set the children out of the way, by the
bread and told the pair of them, who were never
noisy, to be quiet like good children.
"Now Mina," she said "You'll give me a fresh loaf, a
pot of raspberry jam, a half pound of butter and two
pounds of sugar. Oh, and you better give the bairns

one of that things each," and she pointed to the chewy bars.

The older assistant set the groceries on the counter and added them up on a brown paper bag. She was hesitant, yet curious. Looking towards the children she asked, "Is anything wrong with their mother?"

"Losh, lassie, did you not hear then? I should think the whole place knows by now," said Mrs Bethune, packing the goods into her basket.

"What happened?"

"Friday night," Mrs Bethune whispered confidentially, leaning across the counter, "Went for himself with the bread knife. She did a pretty good job on him too. The ambulance and the police were there and the whole place was out too."

She continued to the ashen-faced woman opposite her, "He's home now, but where herself is who knows. He just wants to be left in peace with the bairns."

"And what was it all about?" the serving woman queried. "She looked such a quiet lassie."

"Money, what else," Mrs Bethune almost growled. "That boy was making good money, but I'm thinking it's no on the home or the bairns it was going; seems she couldn't keep away from these party things that they're all having." Mrs Bethune laid her clenched hands on the counter and went on. "She was at one, when he came home. Travelled the length of the country to find a cold home and his bairns on their own. I don't know. Many's the time I offered to keep the bairns if she was wanting out. She was only a young lassie," Mrs Bethune put her hand out for her change and resumed, "When I went in to stay with the bairns when he went to the ambulance, I thought to make them something to eat. Well, Mina, I never saw a house like thon. Not a bite in the place. Do you know what the cupboards were full of? Plastic stuff –

boxes and bowls and jugs with lids on everywhere –
an army couldn't use it. And cane things. Plant pots
and pictures, filling every surface. She could only
start a shop. And you never saw the like of the golden
chains and earrings and what have you. Just lying
about. Well, much good they did her." Mrs Bethune
moved over to the children, handed them a chewy bar
each and wheeled the pushchair towards the door.
She paused and looked straight at the older woman,
"And then of course there was the drink. He told the
public houses not to serve her, I know that. And I
know the shop doesn't give credit," and she eyed the
notice with the large black letters. "With her never
having a halfpenny on her, I know she wasn't getting
it here. But she was getting it somewhere – or from
someone – oh yes, she was getting it somewhere."

P R O G R E S S

The people living on the farm said that you could set
your clock by Tommo. Whatever the season, you'd
see him coming up the road from the village on his
old bike, at the very same time every working day. In
the mornings he passed the row of cottages at exactly
a quarter past seven and it was the same after dinner.
Fifteen minutes before starting time, there he'd be,
belting into the square, large tackety boots pounding
the pedals. He had the hurried gait of a long distance
walker and in whatever he was doing, the anxiety was
apparent in his breast. He asked for nothing and that
is just what he received. I don't think he ever heard of
Worker's Rights. There were some who said that he
wasn't all there, but I think that he was more all there
than most of them saying it.

There were twelve men working on the place when
I arrived fifteen years ago. I used to be grieve on a
farm outside Inverurie. It was a good place but my
wife never really settled to it, so we moved up here to
be near her people.

As on most farms, the men had been there for
many years. I was the incomer, the interloper.
Tommo had served nearly fourteen years by that
time, coming straight into it from school. He was as
strong as an ox and was built to match, his shortish
stout body possessing a fine strength, and he would
work until he dropped. He never drove any of the
machines, he wouldn't have been safe. Unlike even
the youngest boy on the farm, Tommo did not understand the complexities of machinery, which part of it
did what, and his mind was afraid of them.

I hadn't been here for many days when I learned
the reason for this. Trying to keep the bairns of the
village from the shore must have been a little like
trying to turn back the tide: Tommo fell from the
point of the harbour when he was a little fellow. The
tide was out and that saved him, but the rocks were
waiting and he damaged his head. He attended the
village school until he was fourteen, then he got a
start at the farm where his uncle was the cattleman.
He didn't progress above labouring but he knew how
many blue beans made five, as they say up here. He
lived in the village with his sister. She had never
married, whether it was because she hadn't felt inclined, or because of Tommo, no-one could say for
certain.

I hadn't been here long when I learned his worth. I
watched him running across the field, picking up the
big stones before the roller went in. He didn't have to
be told twice to do anything, he'd jump at it with the
willingness of a dumb animal. And when it came to
stacking the bales, there he'd be, trying to do the

whole thing on his own. The others would shout for him to slow down else he'd be killing them. And on the tattie field Tommo would be there again, working at twice the speed of anyone else, snatching the hampers from the squad before they were half filled. Sometimes in his hurry he'd get himself into a bit of a knot, then he'd wave his arms wildly, as if to snap the bands that bound him, and let go with a load of oaths. Myself and Davy especially would then wind him up something awful, watching him become angrier and angrier, tears of frustratuion glimmering in his eyes and the swears falling from his mouth.

In October, when the women came to dress the tatties, the place would be filled with Tommo's loud laughing. The capers that went on then! Above the clattering and banging of the machinery and fork-lift trucks, you'd have to be deaf not to hear the screeching and hilarity that came from them. Tommo'd be the colour of a beetroot at some of the things they'd be saying to him but he enjoyed this time, took his fill of it. And the women were never less than respectful to him and would take him bags of sweeties and good things for his tea. The same crowd had been coming for many years and all knew him well.

I'd been grieve for fifteen years when the big change came. There were many reasons. This could be blamed, that could be blamed. What it came down to in the end was that the farm was being mismanaged and, as usual, it was the working man that had to pay. And so for half of them, their way of life came to a callous and abrupt end.

After we had gathered in that harvest, the boss came to me and told me to inform the men of the shape of things. That half of them were to go, (he hadn't made up his mind just who), but they would be informed on pay day – two days away.

It was a hellish two days. To tell a man that, a man

who had in some cases given two thirds of his life to the same master... and to believe that he did it for wages!

Some found it a harder thing to grasp than others. And there were those who couldn't speak.

I knew it made economic sense. But there are ways to tell a man that he is finished. To have someone you have slaved for for all these years come to you with that and coldly state that the details would be worked out via a solicitor, that someone was coming out to assess their houses, their homes, and a fair rent levied, shook the men and left me with a foul taste in my mouth. I couldn't look into the eyes of the men when I was doing the big man's dirty work. He stood by the door of the shed and chewed at his thumbnail, his eyes on the ground.

There was no such thing as *last on first off* with us. Tommo, with thirty years service behind him and another twenty ahead, was going. No need for labourers, with modern methods. Davy, also with thirty years service was going, got the bullet was how he put it. What young fellow could plough a furrow like Davy? Big Dougie Allen at forty was going. He was the Tommo of the tractormen, another who would work himself into the ground, didn't know when to stop. When Dougie opened his pay packet and found the slip I thought that he was going to drop the boss. He went over to him and stood right in front of him and we could all see the fight that went on in him as he stood there, clenching and unclenching his balled fist.

When himself left, they all rounded on me. And they had the right. Those being kept on shuffled their feet and would look anywhere other than at them going. Davy didn't try to hold himself. It was true what he said, that the big bastard made sure that he got his harvest in first.

I would not like to go through the following three months a second time. Men who had worked closely and well together all these years not speaking to one another, avoiding each other's eyes.' It was as if them going were already gone.

The farming community can be a warm and close-knit place even today. After the redundancies it became a stagnant, moribund place. The earth seemd to fold back in on itself as if it knew what had come upon it.

The men did not find work, and hands which for so long had worked the earth found it hard to lie idle, did not know what to do. Then, about four years later, Tommo found something regular.

After the slump in the oil business, things began to pick up and the local yard was re-employing once more. I was surprised when Eric the shepherd told me that Tommo was working there. Tommo never belonged in that dirty hell-hole of a place. He belonged on the earth whose dirt was of a different kind altogether. With people like himself.

Shortly after he started, I met him in the barber's. He looked just the same old Tommo. The big grin when he saw me coming in, rocking about on the balls of his feet in his hurry to tell me all that was new with him. The words, as ever, tripping over each other in their rush to get from his mouth. He said he was doing fine and indeed he looked it. Being paid off from that place was the best thing that ever happened to him he said. He was free now! A free man. Who wanted to be yoked to the ground all their life? A man was worth more than that, wasn't he? And being thought of as less than the cattle beasts, for they were worth the cash, weren't they. No, he said, he was well out of it. He'd watch the next time that he would be anyone's slave. At this job he got twice what he made on the farm and most of the day he was sitting on his back-side. No, no, from now on he would kill himself for no bugger. You got no medals that way.

I said I agreed with every word he said and that I was glad he got a start, it had been long enough and I wished him all the best and told him to watch himself down there. He laughed at me and poked me in the chest, just like he always used to, then he went out.

It was about three weeks later that a mate of Eric's who worked at the same yard told him that Tommo was dead. He had fallen from the basket carrying the men on to the rig.

The parish was deeply shocked, as it always is to lose one of its own. And accidents in that place were indecently frequent. For long afterwards, little else was talked about.

Tommo's funeral was the biggest seen in these parts since many a day. Not only was the church packed to bursting, but the green outside was overflowing with people. There wasn't a farm in the district but all its men were there and many of the women. We were all there. Except himself. He had bigger and better things to do be doing. For that day he had taken possession of yet another fine farming toy, courtesy of the bank of course. And when the thing defeated him, as they all did, he'd come looking for me. And he'd stand there – chewing his thumbnail.

TEARLACH'S MURDO

On Tuesday Tearlach looked at the sky and decided the day was right for tarring the roof of the house. He went through to the back place to notify his wife of his intention. She paused at the blanket-washing only long enough to tell him to take the dog from under her feet. She'd be falling in the tub with it yet. Tearlach whistled to Murdo and together they went out. Mackay and Donald More had completed their roofs in the two good days they had last week. You could smell the tar through the entire village. Tearlach paused and took his fill of the aroma. Then he shook himself. If he wouldn't shift, the whole place would be beating him...

He was going well. Ach, he'd be done in no time at all. He hoped he'd manage the job without too many distractions. Tearlach might have known different. Dan must have been watching for him. Tearlach was just getting into his stride when he appeared. Could Tearlach have a wee lookie at the outboard? Just when he had the time, mind. When he tried to start her she refused completely. Not a smeeach. Barely lifting his eyes from the roof, Tearlach called down surely. As soon as this lot was finished. Dan was a good enough soul. That he did not understand the first thing about the Seagull engine couldn't be held against him. Tearlach surmised that he must have flooded the thing again. That would be it, Dan shouted up. He'd best let Tearlach get on then, and he went back to his house.

Not many minutes later, Henry Smith appeared. What Henry did not know about everything, and tarring roofs in particular, was not worth the knowing. Aye, but Tearlach was making a start. Man, was he no a wee bit late this year? Mackay and Donald More beat him to it, he saw. Tearlach agreed quietly that that was true enough, they did. Now, did Tearlach no miss a bittie up there – there by the chimley? Tearlach didn't think so but he'd cast his eye over it when he was done. Aye, that would be the thing, said Henry. Awful if he wasn't going to do the thing right. Henry always spoke as if his mouth was filled with pebbles. Either that, or as if he was standing on the sea-bed.

By the time Henry left, the sweat dripping from Tearlach's brow had little to do with his labours, warm though the day was.

He worked without further interruptions for a full half-hour, then Annie put in an appearance. Tearlach sent up a small prayer of thanks towards heaven when she said she would look in on Peggy for a few minutes. Peggy had promised her rhubarb. Lovely the rhubarb Tearlach had. The stalks were as thick as your arm.

By Tearlach's reckoning, Annie spent only long enough in the house to pick up the rhubarb. Then, for twenty minutes at least, she stood at the foot of his ladder imparting all sorts of important information to him. She was just back from the shop. Wasn't it scandalous the price of half a pound of bacon? Tearlach agreed it was awful altogether, and drove himself on. He whistled *'The Barren Rocks of Aden'* a dozen times and Annie was still there, the long stalks of rhubarb sliding from the leaf which Peg had wrapped around them. She was near dead with the toothache last night. Never slept one wink. Saw every hour that was on the clock. She had to put some of her Geordie's whisky on her teeths. Tearlach stopped tarring the same bit over and over and expressed his deep sympathy. The toothache was the very devil. She didn't need to talk to him about toothache. He could still feel the pain from thon big back one the dentist had to pull last summer. No, she needn't talk to him about teeth. That didn't stop her. She talked about Geordie's bad back then. Tearlach was thinking that his front wasn't so very bonnie either. She didn't know when they would get their place done. Geordie's back was that sore with all the work that was waiting on him. Tearlach could believe that. *Stiff Arse* they had called Geordie Smith at the school. Too lazy to get out of his own way. The lassies were better at football than he was. Nothing had changed.

After a bit more about this and that – mainly her total lack of faith in that new doctor who was only a boy and what did he know about people's backs, people moreover, who had their backs for nigh on forty years – Annie left and herself and the rhubarb set out for her house at the end of the street, the small stooped figure in the flowery apron calling out a greeting to all she met on the way.

Tearlach whistled *'The Barren Rocks of Aden'* for the nineteeth time. His was a quiet, tuneless whistle, more an expression of air than a melody. It wasn't true, as his wife said, that it was the only tune he knew. He knew them all. But he liked *'The Barren Rocks...'* It was a nice tune, no, a good tune. It stayed in your head. There were a lot of them like that but *'The Barren Rocks...'* was his favourite.

Tearlach was pleased with his progress. He'd just finish this bit and then he'd see if his wife had the tea ready. What was that gowk of a Henry Smith talking about? There were no bits missed that he could see. He shook his head. Henry always had to be saying something. Satisfied with his work, Tearlach once more took a large breath, inhaling the smell that signalled this season to the village more surely than any calendar.

Tearlach descended the ladder and set the pail of tar on the ground at its foot. Murdo and next door's cat were capering about his ankles. If the two of them wouldn't let be he'd be coped into the bucket of tar. The blessed cat was now tugging at the cuff of his left trouser-leg with Murdo egging it on. Tearlach shook it off. The cat bounded a short distance then returned to vent its spleen on Murdo. It stood four-square, legs spread, spitting fury and then sent a left hook jab-jabbing to Murdo's head. Murdo dared to advance on the enemy. But the big tom was the victor of many wars. No backing away for him from a pesky Scottish terrier of indeterminate age and even more dubious lineage. Its mouth a wide red chasm showing evil fangs, the cat sprang. Murdo, in order to escape this unleashed malevolence, leapt three feet into the air and landed in the pail of tar.

It was difficult to say who looked the most surprised, Tearlach or Murdo. The cat thrust its dish-
face at Tearlach but then, acknowledging the part he
played in the whole fiasco, put his tail between his legs
and slunk away through the lupins, away from sight.

Tearlach looked at Murdo and what used to be
Murdo looked back at Tearlach. Tearlach lifted his
bonnet and scratched the back of his head. He wiped
the sweat from his brow with the back of his hand.
Then he took his hand over his face and rubbed the
back of his neck and uttered a soft 'My faith!'.

"Out you come you little booger. Out from that."

With great difficulty the dog hauled himself from
the pail. Tearlach bent his long frame and looked at
him, astonished at how small his animal appeared.

"Gosh bless me, Murdo, is that you? Is that yourself
my boy?"

For once Tearlach was beat. What now? He
couldn't use the bath. Herself had the blankets in it.
There was nothing else for it. He would have to take
Murdo to the sea, try to scrape as much of the tar as
he could from him that way. But first that pail of tar
had to be moved. What a thing to come on him on
such a promising day. He'd loop the pail over the top
of the ladder until he had his tea, then he'd put the lot
round to the back. He had his foot on the fifth rung
when he heard the scream coming from the house.
He leapt like a boy from where he was, not in the least
concerned now as to the safest place to leave the tar.
He raced into the house, splashed boots entirely forgotten as he stamped over his wife's good rugs.

Tearlach's English wife stood with her back to the
grate, trying, but failing to shoo Murdo away from
her clothes. In his fright Murdo stood on his hind legs
and trailed tar down her stockings and over her
shoes.

"Take him away, Charlie – take him away!" she shrieked. "Put him out!"

Easier said than done. Murdo had eyes everywhere, just like that beast in the Book of Revelations. It would take a wiser man than Tearlach to fool him. The moment Tearlach inched towards him, Murdo dodged round the back of one chair and heaved himself onto another. From there he executed a perfect belly-flop onto the new flowered settee. Tearlach's wife's screams were terrible to hear. He had quite a job quitening her in case the whole toun thought that she was being murdered.

Throwing caution to the four winds, Tearlach piled onto the settee in an effort to entrap the dog, his right foot catching the tablecloth covering the small table there and pulling cloth and photographs and china ornaments onto the floor. His wife had to sit down now. She was quiet and white. Just as Tearlach was about to lay his hand on Murdo, Murdo leapt for the open kitchen door, his tail leaving a wide brush stroke of black on the freshly painted upright. Tearlach, near to tears, picked himself up with difficulty, and once more took off after the offender.

It was with a thankful heart that he saw that the back door was not closed. Tearlach's wife had been backwards and forwards to the blankets and mercifully the thing was hanging wide. Whatever the little mischief would do, it would not be in the house.

Tearlach breathed a deep sigh and went back through to his wife. The poor woman had received a dreadful shock and her just about to call him for his tea.

There was no denying the place was in some state and he had just painted that door last week. His wife was on her feet once more, sufficiently recovered to pour out the tea. She had sorted the small table. Tearlach noticed that a photo of himself baiting the lines had the glass broken and a little dish-lady, that he himself had won at the shows, had her head snapped off. For all that his wife was calm. They both sat there in silence, their grip on their cups as tight as on life itself, trying to ease the turmoil that was in them.

Into this silent state, without knocking, came Ina from next door.

"Tearlach, Tearlach," she beseeched, her dumpling face showing visible signs of distress, "Ow vow, I don't know what to do. Your Murdo was in and the place is all covered with tar. He jumped up onto my mother's lap."

"Is the old one alright?" Tearlach asked, his eyes closed as if to shut out what he felt must be coming.

"Yes, she's alright. She's that blind she thought it was the cat."

"And where's Murdo now? You surely didn't leave him on the old one's lap?" queried Tearlach, taking a life-giving gulp of the black, sweet tea.

"No, not on her lap. Didn't he run out when I took the brush to him. Spraying tar everywhere. Come till you see my palings. My good new paint."

Tearlach had tremendous difficulty in holding himself just then. He wasn't fit for all this. Throwing himself about like an Olympic athlete at his age. All he wanted was to get his roof done and stop Mackay's crowing. He turned his long face towards Ina as he heaved himself to his feet.

"Come then, till I see what you're talking about," and himself and Ina went out through the front door.

Tearlach didn't hear one word of Ina's repetitive tirade on the wickedness of the animal. He saw, right enough, that one or two of her pailings were a wee bit marked, but nothing to send her singing all over the place like that for. If it was tarred pailings that was worrying her, he'd give her something to cry about.

He fetched his pail of tar and, to Ina's perplexity,
instead of taking it to his roof, he set about finishing
the job Murdo had started. One by one, Ina's green
palings with the white points, which she had so
proudly and carefully painted herself only a few days
ago, gave way to a uniform black. Ina couldn't bear to
look and covered her face in her apron. By the time
he was on to the fourth one Tearlach was whistling
'The Barren Rocks of Aden.'

A BIT OF CRACK & CAR CULTURE

"Do you mean to stand there and tell me that a fine-looking fellow like yourself hasn't a girl? I'm no believing that," said Murph, his red watering eyes peering at the young man.

Adam looked up from the wall he was building and drew the back of his hand across his forehead. He acknowledged Murph with a smile and a shake of the head. There was always a lot of good- natured banter going on among the men. The crack was good on the building site.

He knew when they were having him on. He didn't to begin with. He was green then. He came straight from school into this traineeship, where he had learned much more from the brickies and the joiners than ever he was going to learn on release to college, which bored him. For Adam just could not get worked up about sealant joints or fibrous plaster. Instead, he took this learning time off to dream. About the large American car he was going to have one day. A Chevvie, or a fifty-five Chevrolet Bel Air to be right. Some cruiser! Harrison Ford had one in *American Graffiti*. For Adam was a young man, born in the sixties, who did his growing in the seventies and now found himself working in the world of the eighties, and dreaming of the fifties.

Of all the people he worked among, the men who used their hands were the best. They were more on his level and their way was easy. They were men like his father and the men he knew. They were not afraid to dirty their hands; that was where their skills lay and they talked sense. Adam was complicated in that his mind was so sharp that for most of the time it was ahead of him, yet he got no satisfaction from doing anything unless his mind and his hands were in harmony. In this respect he appeared at odds with the rest of the people who worked in the offices of the large firm. He spent the best part of his working days there and an escape to the building site was like breathing in clean air.

"I know," joked Jock, straightening his back from the mixer. "It's that last car. What you need is a nice girl to take your mind from them."

The tall fair fellow was a match for him. "She'd have to be pretty good then," he said, as with one eye closed, he looked along the level of the wall.

"Oh ho, are you hearing that Murph?" the older man asked the one at his back.

Murph was now sitting on a pile of bricks, trying to light his cigarette. The wind was forever gusting in that place they were working in, nearly blinding them with sand. He struck four matches before he had

success. Then he settled back with a loud 'Ah' of
satisfaction. The rest of the squad could see what was
coming. They were long used to Murph and his tales.

"Stop that, till we hear what he's saying," Jock
urged Adam. They downed trowels and gathered
around the seannachaidh. Two others took their
breaths and wandered over to join them. The Nipper
had succeeded in getting the fire going for the tea
and the can was sitting on the flames.

"I mind one girl," began Murph, as the infernal
wind tried to snatch the cigarette from him. "I'd have
been about your own age," he addressed Adam. "Oh
a lovely girl, really lovely. Robina," he dreamed.
"Long black hair right down to her... well right down
her back. She could sit on it."

"What was a bonnie girl like that doing with you,"
scathed Donnie, at the barrow.

"Never you mind that. We were very close Robina
and me. Then she was gone," mourned Murph's
large moon face.

"Och, I'm sorry man. I didn't know about that.
What way did she die?"

"She didn't die. They went off to Aberdeenshire.
Just upped and left in the middle of the night. Like
the mist from the hill. Not a word to a soul. Not even
to myself. And my Robina with them."

"Oh," said Donnie as the light hit him, "I thought
she must have died – for how else could she leave
someone like yourself."

"Naturally. Isn't that what anyone would think?
But, she was one of the Travelling people. They used
to come every October for the tattie picking and
would stay over the winter, though they never came
back after that. Mind, I don't think her father ever
cared that much for me. He used to look at me queer
sometimes." Murph studied his cigarette for a couple
of seconds then drew himself from his reverie and

looked across to Adam. "Ah, my Robina," he said, his heart full.

"You better no let Jessie hear you talking like that," said Donnie, pressing his clasped hands to his breast and pointing his ripped wellington-clad toe from him. "Oh! My Robina!" he mimicked and then turned to the young man beside him. "Now Adam," he warned. "There's a lesson for you. If you land a nice looking one, hold on to her. Otherwise you could end up with an ugly woman," and he let the last two words slide from the corner of his mouth, "like Murph."

"I never saw an ugly woman," stated Jock openly. "I mean a really ugly one."

"No a really ugly one," agreed Murph. "Right enough, you have to admit there's one or two that are maybe no quite so good- looking as others. But no right ugly."

"Well," chipped in Willie Vass who had been silent all this time, apart from when a fit of coughing would grip him. Then whatever was lodged in his chest was fired in any direction, sometimes landing on an innocent rubber boot." I saw one once when I was down in England that nearly made it."

"How? What was she like," queried the Nipper, who was giving an eye to the tea can and the fire.

"Oh really ugly. She kept the place we stayed in, when we went for our holidays. A nice enough woman; she'd give you plenty to eat. But, man, was she ugly." He looked to the assembly for a deeper understanding. "You know what I mean. Ugly." He couldn't seem to get over it.

As one, all eyes turned to him. Willie Vass had little to commend him physically. Too many pints had given him the appearance of an egg on legs. His stature was short and as a result he wobbled like a blancmange when he walked or coughed. His workmates called him Elton on account of his bald head.

His latest was that he was going to the doctor on Saturday to see if he could get a transplant. Jock had been unkind to him already on that score.

"It's no a hair transplant that you're needing. A body transplant would be more the thing." But none of this kind of talk ever put Willie up or down.

The men shifted themselves and re-started work. Adam went back to the office in the centre of the town; he had the men's bonuses to make up.

Going home later in the van, he could hardly hold himself on the seat he was so tired. Across from him the Nipper appeared like something that had come back from the grave; his eyes were red-rimmed and the constant wind had covered him from his feet to his hair in cement and sand. There was however, a large grin on his toothy face.

"Well, Adam my man, I don't know about you, but it's me for the pub the night. Wash some of this sand and stour out of me. As a matter of fact I'll maybe stay there the whole weekend. I feel like getting slowly mortal. Good pay this week," he confided.

"I'll likely end up there sometime, myself," the apprentice nodded. "I'll have a few games of pool, then I'll see."

"Do you take a drammie then?"

"No the hard stuff – I can't take it. My throat closes at the smell of it. No, I usually stick to cider."

"Cider can be potent too if you take enough. What put you off the spirits though?" The Nipper was solicitous in his enquiry.

"Last August I went for the big blitz. I'd spent every minute and penny of four months working on yon car. Ach, I never came out of the shed at all. I nearly destroyed myself. So I just went for it. I drank anything I could get. Then I spewed it all out; I couldn't stop. I can't look at the stuff now."

"Oh well, your mother'll be glad about that,"

nodded the Nipper wisely.

The van rolled homewards, depositing its tired cargo along the way. Murph was the first one to be dropped off. There was the usual 'see you on Monday, Murph' called from them all. Jock shouted after him to watch himself from that one that came to stay next to Geordie Dow – he knew what women were like; a good-looking fellow like himself wasn't safe among them... Murph's reply was drowned in the roar from the van's engine, but his look told Jock plenty.

Donnie's parting words were for Adam.

"Mind now, Adam boy, what I told you. The place is full of lovely girls just looking for a chap like yourself."

"Ay ay, I'm hearing you," Adam raised a grin and waved the older man on his way.

He supposed that he would end up in the bar of the Royal with the rest of the boys. He wasn't in form though. He'd be happier working on the car. She was needing new brake pads. He'd drifted into these weekends and now that they had become ritual, they held little for him. In the beginning it was a new thing. If you took a good drink you were a man. He enjoyed getting to the pool table; he was willing to spend time there perfecting his game, but to put in the entire evening bombed-out in some public house, and see nothing of the lovely nights didn't make sense of any kind to him. Cammy and Yod were quite happy in this state. They looked ahead to always being this way at the end of the week. Maybe, Adam thought, with the passing of time they would get sense.

Sometimes, when he was cruising in his car, the splendour of the nights would take hold of him and he wouldn't want to go to his bed. There was that time in

summer when it never got dark at all and then he'd
feel as if he could reach out and grasp the beauty that
was spread all around him, fold it into himself, merge
with the grandeur. His mother would wonder then
what was keeping him from his home; she thought
that he must be doing dangerous things with the car.
He wasn't that foolish.

Sometimes he wished that he could be more like
the others. Too much in touch with himself, that was
his problem. He recognized this but that didn't alter
anything. He wished he was like Murph. A simplistic
soul and a quiet mind. Had Murph's mother ever said
to him 'Open that door, there's your world'. And, if
she did, what would Murph's answer be? Likely to
take out a cigarette, sit back, and think himself con-
tent enough to be where he was. Or did she take him
on her lap when he was little and fire his mind with
the most wonderful poetry:

Over the mountains of the moon
Down the valley of the shadow
Ride boldly ride, said the sheikh
In search of El Dorado.

He supposed this restlessness came from his mother's
people. On both sides, back through the generations,
there were sea-going men who had seen what was
down that road and over that hill. His mind recoiled
from the prospect of tying himself down with a wife
and babies, like some of those he went to school with.

As he jumped down from the van and called out
his 'See you' to the driver, Adam felt a measure of
calm. He was the last home, he was cold and he was
hungry. His mother would have the big fire going
and his food ready waiting on him. He reckoned he
could put in a couple of hours on the car, then a few
games of pool. Ach, he could see it all coming. He just

wasn't ready yet. That was all... all that he needed was
his time.

OUT TO SEARCH FOR GOLD

After the rain came the rainbow. That it was a sign from God was undisputed by the people of the village. That it appeared on the last Friday of the summer holidays told Davy that it was meant solely for himself and little John.

As is the way in a small fishing village, during the long holidays Davy and little John found themselves many times in the company of the old men who had no work to go to. They would pass their time down by the harbour, yarning and keeping from under the feet of their women. And Davy and little John learnt many things from them. They learnt of the complexities of the Seagull engine, tales of the old days, of mermaids, fairies and other things that they would be better not knowing. Two weeks had passed since they heard the one about the crock of fairy gold. At the end of the rainbow. And they had waited desperately ever since for the rain to come and the rainbow to appear. This wanting rain all of a sudden provoked Davy's mother sorely.

"Rain! Rain! Am I hearing you right? And have you under my feet the entire time and the house full of wet clothes. Now, take an end of this sheet and twist."

Davy did as he was bid, soaking his front as he held the wet blankets against him. His mother had despaired of getting her washing done at all that day. However she had defied the weather and hoped that it would be fair later on. To see her bedding spread before heaven on the whins, drying and bleaching in the sun filled her with a deep satisfaction.

Davy hated washing day in any case, but the yearly blanket washing was in all probability the foulest time that was ever in it as far as he was concerned. For a start it meant that he was pretty much confined to the house, as the water had to be lifted from the well which was in the park at the back of their house. When he wasn't going there he was coming back. All day this went on. His mother used a vast amount of water.

Of course Davy would leave the well with two buckets that were filled right to the brim. By the time he entered the back kitchen, between the two pails there was barely enough for a cat to drink. He'd begin the journey slowly, taking the utmost care that on this particular occasion he would not spill one drop. And he'd manage that, for a few yards. But as his pride in his skill as a water carrier grew, so too did the desire to have the thing over and done with. Slowly the bare brown legs in the worn sandshoes gathered momentum, heels pushed into the grass, knees slightly dipped to withstand the strain. Quicker and quicker became his steps, gradually his stride lengthened. With the increased gait the buckets would bump against him, water gushing onto the grass and over Davy's feet, escaping through the holes at the toes. Tired of the whole affair and frustrated yet again in his brave attempt to do the thing right, Davy gave up altogether and the last part of his trek was performed at something resembling a gallop, surprising his mother's neighbour who was already spreading her sheets, and the farmer's old horse who lived in the field.

His mother's response to Davy's well-meant endeavours never varied. "It's blankets I'm washing, not a teaspoon. You'll have to go for more." And to the look he gave her, which was a mixture of resigned defeat and rebellion, "And you can straighten your face before you leave the house."

Today, luck was with Davy. It had been raining ceaselessly from the previous evening and now at two in the afternoon the place was dry. Davy, much to his mother's delight and bafflement, kept away from her the whole day. Anchored on the sofa beneath the window he kept a relentless watch on the weather, now praying that the rain would stop and that a rainbow would appear.

Of course it did. He squealed the news to his mother, startling her in mid-spit as she tested the heat of the flat iron. The spittle sizzled on the hot surface and ran over the side of the iron, disappearing completely, somewhere between it and the floor.

"I'll have to go now," Davy said. "Little John'll be waiting for me."

"And what about my water?" His mother was hot and cross-looking with the heat from the fire and the iron. She thudded the heavy iron down on a pair of his father's dungarees.

"Aw, Ma," Davy groaned. "John'll be waiting."

"And what's the big hurry all of a sudden? I dare-say little John will wait a little longer."

"Aw, Ma, the rainbow's out." Davy sounded as if some form of torture were being carried out on him. "It'll likely be away by the time I get out of this house," Davy's voice had changed into a querulous girn. "And me waiting for it for weeks," he was almost crying.

"Right," his trauchled mother said as she folded the dungarees and added them to the neat pile. "Be going. But mind, you'll go to the well when you come back."

"I will Ma. Honest Ma."

"And be sure to look after that bairn," she called to his back as he slid through the door.

Little John was sitting on his doorstep waiting for Davy. It surprised him that his mother had agreed to his going out. She was inclined to protect him over-much. He'd been complaining of a sore stomach for the past week and she was loath to leave him out of her sight. She knew, none better, that the minute he escaped from the house, he'd head to the shore and the rocks. There wasn't a time but he came home soaked through from the feet to the waist. When she asked why this was, he never failed to look totally surprised, making her wonder if he knew what he was at half the time. For little John lived almost entirely in his own imagination. In a world of giants and mermaids and pots of gold. Old Johndy and the others were great storytellers, and when he wasn't on the shore little John was with them, listening to all sorts of tales. And what he did not find out from old Johndy he learnt from his own father who had a few stories of his own.

Little John could still taste the Syrup of Figs his

mother insisted he take before she would let him out of the house. He pushed his spittle around in his mouth, forcing it up into his cheeks, making them bulge. Then he washed it around his gums and through his teeth. He did this many times, swallowing with difficulty. He screwed his eyes shut and gave a fierce shudder. Then he rubbed the flat of his left hand up and down on his bottom lip, as if to wipe away the taste.

He had a kype with him, not daring to take his father's good spade. A kype started out as a spade. It was flattened and rounded and was used for digging lugworms. Its handle was long.

From a long way off little John saw Davy coming. He was the only one on the road and he bounded along, his large feet thumping the surface. From that distance little John could make out that he was carrying a bag of some sort. He surmised that it would be for carrying the gold.

As Davy drew near he called out to little John.

"Boy, I never thought she would let me out. Was yours alright?"

"She was alright, but she made me drink a half bottle of Syrup of Figs before she let me go. I hate Syrup of Figs. I'm going to die with it yet," little John said as he rose to his feet.

The two boys set out. One was large for his years and everything about him was the colour of the earth. The other was a small boy, washed to paleness, it seemed, by the sea. Through the village street they walked, the small viking carrying a kype, like some diminutive warrior setting out for a battle, and the brown boy with the rolled up sack tucked beneath his arm. Davy's strides were long, little John took short running steps to keep abreast of him.

They saw no-one until they came to the last house

in the village. Drawing near to it was Hughag, who
was returning from the shore, a hundredweight of
welks wedged beneath the bar of her ramshackle old
bicycle. She was well up in years but was still a strong
hardworking woman. Large and heavy, she had a
kind smiling face that was always turned towards her
neighbour and especially to all children. Although
the weather was very warm Hughag was clad in many
jumpers, two skirts and a tweed jacket tied with a
piece of rope. On her feet she wore men's heavy
wellington boots. Her only concession to summer lay
in the fact that she had discarded the army greatcoat
which in the colder weather covered her from the
neck very nearly to her toes. A brown balaclava
covered her sparse white hair, and a scarf that was
long enough and thick enough to tie up a boat was
wound round her neck many times. No-one could
remember seeing Hughag dressed any other way; the
question was often asked just how much was layers of
clothing and how much was Hughag. She was a spin-
ster and lived alone since her mother died.

When she saw Davy and little John she hailed them
pleasantly. Leaning the bike against the garden dyke
she stood a while to regain her breath.

"You're just the very fellows I'm looking for," she
panted as they drew level.

"I'm wanting you to look for mice for me." At their
blank stares she elaborated. "I have them. Come on in
with me till I show you."

Going into Hughag's house was like stepping from
the daylight into darkness. The small window which
should have afforded light to the room had a dark
gray net curtain draped diagonally across it. The
small panes were coated in a dirty brown sticky depo-
sit that came from the blowback from Hughag's fire
and the pollution from her pipe. The fact that neither
curtain nor glass had seen water for many years did

not help matters.

"I'm wanting you to look in that press over there," Hughag said as she stood inside the door, Davy and little John close behind her. She moved over to the press, wading through piles of old yellowing newspapers, porage oat packets and cocoa tins, scattering two white hens from their roost on the back of the sofa as she passed.

As Davy followed her, little John held back by the door, his hands pressed to his thighs to protect himself from the hens. "Look you now," Hughag urged Davy as he peered into the darkness below. "Down there on the bottom," she directed, and she doubled herself to look in with him.

"I canna see anything," said Davy, withdrawing and looking up into Hughag's creased face.

"Well, what's that?" Hughag queried, and she thrust a packet of munchmallows right under Davy's nose. "Look you," and she pointed to the part of the packet through which some small thing had chewed, right through to the silver wrapper and through that to the soft chocolate mallows.

"I have stuff down, but I think they're only eating it. Look in that green saucer. There's droppings there alright but no a sign of the little mischiefs. Are you sure you're seeing nothing?" she asked Davy, whose knees were beginning to ache. Davy rose and shook his head. "There's nothing there," he said. "As sure as death," and he edged towards the door and little John.

Hughag's voice arrested him as he was negotiating the cocoa tins and coal pails.

"And where's the two of you off to the day, this last day of your holidays?"

Davy told her.

"Well I'm blessed. Do you know that many have looked, but no-one has ever found anything. Not even a brass farthing. I don't know but you'll be the fellows to do it."

"Me and John's going to find it," Davy said grandly. "We'll be the first people that ever found the pot of gold," he threw at her from the doorway.

Little John said nothing. He looked at Hughag and folded back into himself still more.

"I was just thinking," said Hughag, crossing the room to the grate. "If you're going all that way you'd be the better of something in your bellies," and she took the poker and roused the fire. Then she swung the kettle onto the flames. "Sit you there," she nodded to the sofa which was covered completely in ancient copies of the *Christian Herald*. "Slide that lot on to the floor."

Davy and little John came unwillingly. Davy plonked himself heavily in the centre and crossed his arms across his chest, sighing audibly. Little John perched on the edge, near to Davy, and was quiet. He still wasn't sure about the hens and he bent low and clasped his arms around his legs. Davy's sighing changed note and became a tuneless humming.

"What's bothering you, Davy Mackay?" Hughag looked up from scattering a handful of tea-leaves into the pot.

"We should be going," Davy answered. "The rainbow might go away on us."

"Not it" laughed Hughag. "Losh bless me boy, it's just out. Is it going to go in right away then? Not it," she repeated, and she poured the boiling water on to the leaves and set the pot to the side of the fire.

She took two cups from the press and blew the dust from them. Then she took the hem of one of her skirts around the inside. Davy's left foot tapped out a quiet tattoo on the gray linoleum, keeping time with his humming. Little John twisted himself into knots, inside and out.

After handing them their tea, with a large piece of bannock spread thickly with margarine and rhubarb jam, Hughag sat down in her high-backed chair by the fire.

The two of them did their best. Little John's stomach, so newly exposed to an overlarge dose of Syrup of Figs, revolted completely at the generous chunks of rhubarb and the substantial amount of ginger which Hughag added to the jam.

As Hughag drank her tea she seemed to have forgotten for a short while that she was entertaining two guests. Her head was sunk on her chest and Davy and little John guessed that she had gone to sleep on them. They were wondering how to break the heavy silence which they felt in the room, when she raised her head and looked across to them.

"You know that's the fairy gold you're going after. Well, as you're nearing the end of the rainbow be sure and keep your eyes open wide. For wherever they are, the gold is sure to be. They'll lead you straight to it."

"Did you ever see the fairies?" breathed little John at last.

"No meudail. But I heard a story of a man that did."

"Is he from Hilltown?"

"He was. Oh, many, many years ago I'm talking about."

"He didn't find the gold did he?" put in Davy, deeply concerned.

"No. But he danced with the fairies. Put your cups on that chair and Hughag'll tell you a story that you maybe haven't heard before." Hughag drained her own cup and placed it on the floor by her feet. "Now then," when she was certain that she had their attention. "You know Finlay Dearg?" she asked of them.

"Is that Finlay that lives beside the shop?" little

John asked while Davy nodded.

"That's him. Now, in the olden days there was another man of that name. He was that Finlay's great grandfather."

"Was he old?" queried little John.

"Not very old. Not then," Hughag replied. "Now, one day, it was the day after there had been a wild sea storm, this Fionnlagh Dearg was along the shore looking for his clighs that had been washed up. He walked far."

"Right over to Skaravak?" Davy piped up.

"Oh, farther than that. Away past the summerhouse."

"That's miles," Davy stressed.

"You don't need to tell me. Anyway, back in them days tinker folk used to camp over there. They'd stay in the cave in the cliffs. They'd be gathering the whelks."

"Just like you," Davy said.

"You're correct, Davy. Well, this day, as I've said already, Fionnlagh Dearg had wandered far looking for his creels. And his feet were that sore with walking over the stones and the rocks and he was hungry."

"My father looks for his clighs when they're wrecked," said little John.

"He does," Hughag agreed. "Many's the time I meet him. Now, Fionnlagh's away far from his home. His belly's thinking that his throat's cut and he's thinking to himself 'If I continue for a short distance maybe the tinkers will give me a bite.' Very kind people," Hughag allowed. "They'd give you what was theirs; so Fionnlagh was right enough there," she nodded confidentially to Davy and little John. "Anyhow, to cut a longish story short, seeing that you have to be going far, he went up to the camp where they treated him like one of their own and soon there was not a word about hunger or sore feet."

"We better be going," Davy told Hughag, half rising.

"Was the fairies in the tinkers camp," asked little John.

"No. Not then. But the tinkers liked Fionnlagh that much that they pressed him to stay until the next day. One of their girls was getting married, do you see."

Davy and little John nodded that they did.

"Did they all sleep in the cave?" Davy asked.

"Indeed, and I don't know. But the story is that Fionnlagh stayed. And a wedding the like of it was never seen nor heard of. The food – where they got it from, who knew? Everything they had. Sheep, hens, salmon. Everything. And whisky. Enough to fill the pond up the back. And the music. Fionlagh said thay he had never heard piping like it and he was some piper himself. Then the lovely girl that was the bride took the pipes from her father and began to play. So sweet was her playing, said Fionnlagh Dearg, that out from the side of the cliff marched a band of fairies, a little piper at their head."

Davy was incredulous. Little John was spellbound. Hughag took her breath. "His pipes would be awful little," Davy said.

"He would have little hands," little John was helpful.

"And then the dancing began to get really wild. For if the tinker people could play, this little fellow's playing came from the realms of glory itself. Fionnlagh Dearg was dancing good style, leaping and throwing himself about all over the place, the little fairies weaving in and out beneath his feet."

"It's a wonder he didn't stamp on them, eh?" asked Davy, shifting his bare thighs on the horse hair sofa.

"What size were they?" asked little John.

"Oh, you know what size fairies are. Fionlagh Dearg swore that this ones were the size of whisky bottles. There were those who said that it was what was in the bottles that had more to do with it," and Hughag laughed chestily with mirth.

"Did he go into the cliff with the fairies?" little John asked, ignoring the kick that Davy gave to his ankle as a signal for them to leave.

"I don't know about that. I've never heard it mentioned. He may have for all anyone knew. All the people knew was that he went out looking for his clighs on the Tuesday and it was the following Tuesday before he walked into his house."

"Did he get his clighs?" Davy asked.

"No, no clighs. And his poor wife near to losing her wits thinking that the sea took him."

"We better be going," said Davy loudly as he edged towards the door. "Thanks for the tea."

"Thanks for the tea," said little John shyly, scampering after Davy.

"Don't go yet. I have something for you. There," Hughag said benevolently as she bestowed on them the chewed packet of munchmallows. "For your piece."

Once clear of Hughag's house, Davy and little John raced away to the park and while little John looked carefully about to ensure that there was no-one about, Davy pitched the munchmallows as hard as he could on to the shore. They left them there, floating in a pool.

The rainbow was still in the sky. After what seemed to him a very long march, little John's steps began to drag. The kype became heavy and cumbersome. The fair head drooped as his short legs hurried to keep up with Davy. The seagulls whirled about the cliffs towering high above them, and the sea settled to a mirror of glass. The black tarred fisherman's bothy, with the large anchors lying in front of it was behind them and the end of the rainbow was near.

"We're nearly there," Davy comforted little John. "Just at the back of that trees."

"I'm glad. My legs are sort of sore."

"Ach, you'll soon get a rest man. No long now. Give me the kype and you can take the bag."

Beyond the trees the rainbow still went on.

Davy was dismayed. Little John was spent. The summer house sat four square of solid stone, tucked in beneath the cliff.

"What are we going to do now, Dave?"

Davy wasn't dismayed for very long. "I know. There's the summer house. Coming to look for the fairies?"

"Do you think we should?"

"Come on," the big fellow urged. "They're bound to be in there."

They sped with heart stopping urgency to the foot of the rock.

"Are you in there, fairies?" Davy boomed, jabbing at the rock with the handle of the kype, while the cliff threw his voice back to him. Little John had difficulty in keeping his balance on a round boulder. Bravely pulling aside a whin bush, he repeated Davy's question politely, "Are you in there little fairies?"

"Come on out," Davy shouted. "We're not frightened of you."

Little John grew daring. "Ha, ha ha," he said. "You can't catch me for a bumble bee," and he raced away from the cliff, slowing to small hops and skips when he was well clear.

Davy threw down the challenge. "Come out here and I'll take on four thousand of you with one hand," was his boast.

"Don't be frightened little fairies," little John contradicted him, "No-one's going to harm you."

Then Davy made the sound of the pipes with his mouth and marched around in a circle while his fingers played an imaginary chanter.

"I think I'm getting frightened Dave," said little John. "What if they get us?"

"Ach, who cares?" said Davy with huge bravado. "They're only the size of your creenie. We could put the whole lot of them in that bag," and once more he bellowed to the rock while it repeated his question hollowly. "Look," he pressed little John, "We'll tear the bushes away with the kype. Then we'll know if there's a crack or anything that they can get through."

They battered the bush. They sliced and tore at it. They broke sweat doing it but all to no avail. The bush still grew, strong, prickly and everywhere. And when little John straightened, his breath almost stopped in him.

"Davy," he whispered to Davy's back, as Davy took strong determined swipes with the kype. He shook Davy's kype arm. "The rainbow's away Davy."

When Davy looked into the sky, little John thought at first that he was going to cry. He'd never seen Davy cry. He cried. Everyone knew that. But Davy? Never.

"Oh, well," said Davy, the disappointment dripping from him. "Oh well," and he threw the kype to his feet. "I was sure it was at the back of the trees," and his lower lip trembled alarmingly. "I don't expect we'll ever get the gold now."

On seeing Davy's crumpled state little John bravely overcame his initial disappointment. "Yes we will, Dave. Yes we will. Remember what old Hughag said," he urged his friend. "No-one has ever found it. That means it is still there. The next time we come we'll not stop for anything. If anyone sees us we'll run down the shore way. We'll just go straight as anything to the end of the rainbow. We'll find it Dave, I know we will."

At little John's optimism, Davy gradually

brightened. Slowly his own spirit came back into him. He said:

"And when we're old, or even when we're dead, people will be saying, 'Do you mind Davy Mackay and John Sinclair? They were the ones that found the pot of gold that the fairies hid," and Davy's eyes took on a far-off look as they lifted to heaven. Yes, he could see it. Of course he still had to master the skill of drawing and ferrying two full pails of water from the well. The way he was feeling now, he had every confidence that he would manage that as soon as he got home.

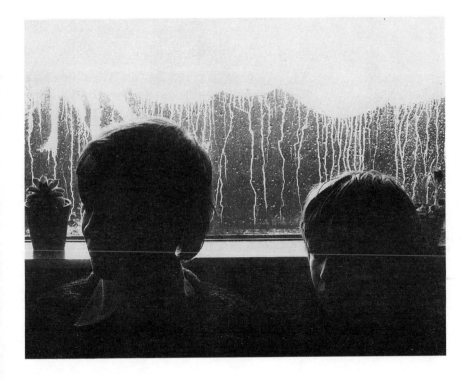

The photographs in this book were taken in Shetland, Orkney and the Faroes, and two have appeared previously in films – *'Ill Fares the Land'* and *'Andrina'*.

OTHER TITLES FROM BALNAIN BOOKS INCLUDE:

Nyakim's Windows Stanley Robertson
illustrated by Simon Fraser   paperback £9.95
The master story-teller's own original stories of the Traveller people:
bizarre happenings, warmth and humour – with more than a hint of the
supernatural! Written in easily-read Scots.

'Magical Mysteries...formidable literary artistry'. *Hamish Henderson   The
Scotsman*

Exodus to Alford Stanley Robertson
illustrated by Simon Fraser   paperback £7.95
Stanley Robertson's highly popular first book appeared on two best-seller
lists.

'...if Exodus to Alford fails to hold your attention, a new wonder has
befallen the human race...' *Books in Scotland*
'...fabulous book..' *The Scotsman*

In Symphony Austere Richard Frere
illustrated by Eric Ritchie   paperback £7.95
Richard Frere, well-known author and man of the hills. '..emergence of
the author's love of the hills...worthy of careful reading..' *Martin Moran
The Scots Magazine*

'If a humble walker should ever want to understand why a man climbs,
then start here...' *Country Walking*

A Celebration for Magnus George Mackay Brown
fully illustrated   £7.95
The celebrated Orkney writer recreates the story following the death of
the earl and saint; interwoven with musical scoring by Peter Maxwell
Davies, plus rich visual imagery.

'...a beautiful book, both visually and verbally...' *Alan Bold   The Scotsman*

The Loom of Light George Mackay Brown
illustrated by Gunnie Moberg, and Simon Fraser   £5.95
'...the life of Magnus is a legend that illuminates the modern world...illus-
trations perfectly complement the play...' *Alan Bold   The Scotsman*

for a complete catalogue contact the publishers:
Balnain Books, Lochloy Road, Nairn IV12 5LF Scotland

to order direct in the U.K., enclose cover price plus 20% to
cover post and packing.